THE HIDDEN FLAME

THE HIDDEN FLAME

BRYAN HEWES

SLICKHILL MEDIA
WWW.SLICKHILLMEDIA.COM

Slickhill Media Publishingwww.slickhillmedia.com

ISBN: 979-8-218-91006-8

10 9 8 7 6 5 4 3 2 1
FIRST EDITION

Printed in the United States of America

DEDICATION

For all those who carry a hidden flame within them,
waiting for the moment to let it shine.

WESTERN SEA
THE CAPITAL
HIGHS PINE
PINEWILD
Coastal Village
THE ASH CAVES
IRONHOLD

CHAPTER 1

THE EGG IN THE SNOW

The wind from the sea carried the smell of salt and pine, and something else beneath it, something that made the hairs on Lina's arms stand on end even before she reached the cliff's edge. She crouched low against the granite outcrop, pressing her body into the cold stone, and watched the figure moving along the narrow path below.

Finn walked with his shoulders loose and his hands open at his sides, his light hair catching the weak afternoon sun, and he moved toward the ridge where the dragon waited as if he were strolling to the village well for water. The creature was twice the length of a fishing boat, its scales the color of cooling embers, and it had been circling the cliffs for three days now while the village huddled in fear behind barred doors. Everyone knew what happened when dragons came.

Everyone knew what King Brann's hunters did to them. But Finn walked closer, and the dragon did not run, and Lina found she had stopped breathing altogether.

She should not be here. Her mother thought she was gathering driftwood along the shore, and the shore was a safe place, a sensible place, far from the clifftops where dragons perched and hunters patrolled.

Lina had seen Finn leaving the village at dawn, and she had seen the direction he took, and something had pulled at her chest until her feet followed. Now she pressed her cheek against the rock and watched him approach the dragon with nothing in his hands, no weapon, no net, no chain.

The creature's head swung toward him, nostrils flaring, and a sound came from its throat that was not quite a growl. Lina's fingers dug into the stone. The dragon's eyes caught the light and held it, amber and depthless, and its tail swept once across the ground, scattering loose shale down the cliff face.

Finn stopped. He was close enough now that one snap of those jaws would end him, close enough that the heat from the dragon's breath must be warming his face. He did not raise his hands or speak or step back. He stood still, and the dragon stood still, and the wind howled between them, carrying salt and pine and that strange burning scent that Lina now understood was the dragon itself.

Seconds passed. The creature's head lowered, just slightly, and its wings folded tighter against its body. Finn took one step closer. The dragon's nostrils flared again, testing the air, testing him, and then it made a sound Lina had never heard from any living thing, a low rumbling tone that seemed to vibrate through the stone beneath her hands. Finn raised one arm slowly, palm forward, and the dragon's head moved toward it until the scales of its snout brushed against his fingers.

Lina's chest ached. She realized she had been holding her breath for far too long and let it out in a rush that fogged in the cold air. The dragon's head turned toward the sound, those amber eyes scanning the clifftop, and Lina pressed herself flatter against the stone until her ribs protested. For a moment nothing moved.

Finn's voice drifted up to her, soft and steady, words she could not make out but which seemed to draw the dragon's attention back to him. Its head swung away from her hiding place, and it let out a breath that sent a plume of heat shimmering into the grey sky. Finn's hand remained on its snout, steady as stone, and Lina watched his lips move in what looked like a low continuous murmur. The dragon's eyes were half-closed. Its body, which had been coiled tight as a ship's rope, began to settle.

She had heard stories of this, old stories that her grandmother used to tell before the king's men burned her collection of carved tablets and warned her never to speak of the old ways again. Stories of humans and dragons living alongside one another, of bonds formed through patience and trust rather than chains and fire. Lina had thought they were just stories.

She had thought the only relationship between humans and dragons was the one enforced by hunters and executioners, the one built on fear and ended in ash. But Finn stood with his hand on a dragon's snout, and the dragon did not burn him, and the stories suddenly felt less like dreams and more like memories half-forgotten.

The afternoon light was fading by the time Finn stepped back, and the dragon spread its wings. The sound of those wings unfurling was like sails catching a gale, a crack and a rush of displaced air that made Lina duck instinctively. The creature launched itself from the cliff in a single powerful thrust, and for a moment its shadow passed over her, vast and dark and warm. Then it was rising, climbing toward the clouds, and Finn stood alone on the ridge with his head tilted back to watch it go.

Lina stayed pressed against her hiding spot until the dragon was nothing but a dark speck against the grey, until Finn had turned and begun walking back toward the village path. Then she rose on shaking legs and brushed the stone dust from her clothes, and she took a different route home so that no one would know where she had been.

Back at home, the evening meal was thin fish soup and hard bread, the same as every evening meal for as long as Lina could remember. Her mother sat across from her, spooning broth into her own mouth with the motions of someone whose mind was elsewhere, and Lina pushed her own food around the wooden bowl without appetite.

The dragon's eyes kept appearing in her thoughts, amber and depthless, and the sound it had made, that low rumbling tone that had vibrated through the stone. She had felt something when she watched Finn approach the creature. She had felt something when their eyes met and the dragon chose not to attack. It was not fear, or not only fear. It was something else. Something that sat on her chest and would not settle.

"You're quiet tonight," her mother said, and Lina realized she had been staring at the same piece of bread for several minutes.

"Tired," Lina said, which was true enough. "The driftwood was scattered far down the shore."

Her mother nodded without looking up. The lie sat heavy in Lina's stomach, heavier than the soup. She had never been good at deception, had never needed to be before today. But she knew, without quite understanding why, that what she had seen on the cliff was not something she could share. Not with her mother, who flinched at every mention of dragons. Not with anyone in the village, where fear of the king's hunters ran deeper than fear of the creatures themselves.

After the meal she helped wash the bowls and stoke the fire, and then she lay in her narrow bed and listened to the wind rattling the shutters. Sleep would not come. Every time she closed her eyes she saw Finn's hand rising, saw the dragon's head lowering, saw that moment of contact when everything she had been told about dragons was proven false.

She heard her grandmother's voice drifting in from memory, speaking words that had been forbidden for a decade now. *Fire does not only destroy. Fire also warms.* Lina pulled her blanket tighter and stared at the darkness above her bed, and the wind kept howling, and the night stretched on.

She woke before dawn without remembering falling asleep. Grey light was seeping through the cracks in the shutters, and the house was cold, and the fire had burned down to embers. Lina dressed quickly in the darkness, pulling on her warmest clothes and the leather boots that had been her father's before the sea took him. She told herself she was going to check the fishing lines. She told herself she needed air. But her feet carried her past the shore and up the winding path toward the mountains, and she did not try to stop them.

The path grew steeper as it climbed away from the village, cutting through dense pine forest before emerging onto bare rock. Lina had come this way before, gathering mushrooms in autumn and pinecones for kindling, but she had never climbed so high or gone so far from the routes she knew.

The sun crept above the horizon as she walked, painting the sky in shades of pink and gold, and the wind grew colder as she gained elevation. She pulled her cloak tighter and kept climbing. She did not know what she was looking for. She knew only that she could not stay in the village another day without understanding what she had seen.

Nearby, an entrance to a cave was hidden by an overhang of rock and a tangle of dead brush, and Lina would have walked right past it if she had not stopped to catch her breath at exactly the wrong moment. Or perhaps the right moment.

The wind shifted, and she caught that scent again, the burning smell that was not quite smoke, and she turned toward it before her mind had finished recognizing what it was. The cave mouth was barely wide enough for her to squeeze through, the rock scraping at her shoulders as she pushed past the brush and into darkness.

For a moment she could see nothing. Then her eyes adjusted, and a faint glow became visible deeper in the cave, an orange light that flickered against the stone walls. Her heart was beating too fast. Her hands were shaking. She should turn back, she knew. She should leave this place and forget she had ever found it and return to her life of fish soup and driftwood and fear. But her feet carried her forward, step by careful step, and the light grew brighter, and the warmth grew stronger, and then the passage opened into a wider chamber and she stopped.

An abandoned egg sat nested in a bed of ash and char. It was the size of her head, perhaps larger, and its surface glowed with an inner fire that pulsed in a slow rhythm. Veins of gold ran through the dark shell, and where the light caught them, they seemed to move, seemed to flow beneath the surface. Lina's breath caught in her throat.

She had never seen a dragon egg before. No one in the village had. The king's hunters destroyed every egg they found, smashed them before the creatures inside could hatch and grow into threats. But this egg was whole and warm and alive, its pulse steady as a heartbeat, and no hunter had found it yet.

She knelt beside it without deciding to kneel. Her hand reached toward its surface without hesitation. The shell was warm beneath her fingers, warmer than she had expected, and smooth except for the raised veins of gold that traced patterns across its surface.

She pulled her hand back, her breath coming fast and shallow, and stared at the egg as if it might hatch at any moment. It did not. The light continued its slow pulse, steady and patient, and the chamber remained silent except for the distant howl of wind at the cave's entrance.

Lina sat back on her heels and wrapped her arms around herself. She should tell someone. She should report this to the village elder, who would report it to the patrol, who would send word to the hunters, who would come and destroy the egg before whatever was inside could threaten anyone. That was what a good citizen of King Brann's realm would do. That was what she had been taught to do since before she could remember.

Dragons were dangerous. Dragons were chaos. Dragons had to be destroyed before they destroyed everything else. But the egg pulsed with light, warm and alive, and Lina thought of the dragon on the cliff, of its head lowering toward Finn's hand, of the sound it made that was not anger or threat but something else entirely.

The sun was low in the sky by the time she emerged from the cave. She had been inside for hours, she realized, sitting in the warmth of the chamber and watching the egg's slow pulse and thinking thoughts that felt dangerous even inside her own head.

Now the wind cut through her cloak and reminded her that the world outside was cold, hungry, afraid, and she had responsibilities waiting in the village, and she could not spend her days hiding in mountain caves with forbidden things. She looked back once at the hidden entrance, memorizing its position against the rock face, and then she began the long walk home.

She did not tell anyone about the egg. She helped her mother mend fishing nets and prepared dinner and answered questions about her day with lies that came easier than they should have. And that night, lying in her narrow bed with the wind howling outside, she decided. The king's hunters would not find the egg. Whatever was growing inside that shell, whatever life was waiting to emerge, it would not be smashed and scattered and forgotten. Lina did not know how to care for a dragon.

She did not know how to keep such a secret in a village where everyone watched everyone else and fear made informants of neighbors. But she knew that she could not simply do nothing. She knew that walking away from that cave and pretending she had never found it was not something she could live with.

The egg was alone, hidden, and alive, and now it was hers to protect.

Chapter 2

FIRST BREATH

A storm rolled in from the sea on the first morning, battering the village with rain and wind that made the fishing boats strain against their moorings and kept everyone indoors mending nets and patching roofs.

Lina sat by the fire with her mother and listened to the rain hammering the old thatch above them, and her thoughts drifted constantly to the mountain, to the hidden chamber, to the egg.

She imagined the storm finding the cave entrance, water pouring in to drown the fire that kept the egg alive. She imagined hunters stumbling across it while seeking shelter from the weather. She imagined the shell cracking open to emptiness and silence, the life inside extinguished before it ever began. Her hands trembled as she worked the fishing nets, and when her mother asked if she was cold, Lina lied and said yes.

On the second day the rain eased but the wind remained, howling down from the mountains with a biting edge that kept the villagers close to their hearths. Lina's mother sent her to the village well for water, and she passed Finn on the path, his light hair damp and his expression distant. He nodded to her without speaking, the way he always did, and Lina wondered what he would say if he knew what she had found.

Would he help her protect it, the way he had protected the dragon on the cliff? Or would he tell her she was foolish, that one girl could not hide a dragon from the king's hunters, that she should report the egg and forget she had ever seen it? She did not know him well enough to guess. She filled her bucket and carried it home, and the wind pushed her back the whole way as if urging her toward the mountains.

The third day dawned clear and cold, the sky scrubbed clean by the storm and the air sharp enough to hurt her lungs. Lina told her mother she was going to gather pinecones in the forest, a task that would explain a full day's absence if anyone thought to ask. She packed bread and dried fish in a cloth bundle, filled a waterskin, and set out before the sun had fully risen above the sea.

The path to the mountains was muddy from the rain, slick in places where the ground had not yet dried, and she moved carefully, testing each step before committing her weight. She could not afford a twisted ankle or a fall that would leave her injured and helpless on the mountainside. The egg needed her. Whatever was growing inside that shell needed someone to keep it safe, and there was no one else.

The cave entrance was harder to find than she remembered, the dead brush that concealed it scattered by the storm and the overhang of rock dripping with moisture. But the scent was still there, that burning smell that was not quite smoke, and she followed it through the narrow gap in the stone until the darkness swallowed her. For a moment she stood still, letting her eyes adjust, her heart beating too fast in her chest. What if the egg had died? What if the storm had reached it somehow, or a predator had found the cave, or the life inside had simply given up waiting for warmth that never came? She forced herself to move forward, one hand trailing along the damp stone wall, and the faint orange glow appeared ahead of her, and she let out a breath she had not realized she was holding.

The egg sat where she had left it, nested in its hollow of ash and char, its surface pulsing with that slow warm light. But something had changed. The pulse was faster now, stronger, and the veins of gold that traced the shell seemed brighter, more defined. Lina knelt beside it and placed her hand on its surface, and the warmth that met her palm was greater than before, almost hot, as if the fire inside was building toward something. She could feel a vibration beneath her fingers, faint but steady, and she realized with a start that it was not the egg itself that was vibrating. It was something inside. Something moving.

"You're still alive," she whispered, and the vibration beneath her hand seemed to quicken in response. The shell was warm enough now that she had to shift her grip, moving her palm to a cooler spot, and the light pulsed brighter for a moment before settling back to its steady rhythm. Lina sat back on her heels and studied the egg, her mind racing through possibilities. She could not leave it here. The cave was too exposed, too easy to find for anyone who knew these mountains. And if the egg was going to hatch, if whatever was inside was going to emerge into a world that wanted it dead, then it needed somewhere safer. Somewhere hidden. Somewhere she could reach without climbing for half a day.

The Pinewild Forest stretched between the village and the mountains, dense and dark and largely avoided by the villagers who feared what might lurk beneath its canopy. Lina had ventured into its edges before, gathering mushrooms and deadfall for kindling, but she had never gone deep. There were old paths in there, her grandmother had told her once, paths that led to shelters built by people who lived in Frostmark before the king's laws made everyone afraid. Most of those shelters had collapsed long ago, claimed by weather and neglect, but some remained standing, hidden beneath the evergreen branches where the sunlight never reached. If she could find one of those shelters, if she could make it safe and warm enough for the egg, then she might have a chance of keeping it hidden until she could figure out what to do next.

Moving the egg was harder than she had anticipated. It was heavier than it looked, dense and solid and awkward to grip, and she had to wrap it in her cloak and carry it pressed against her chest to keep from dropping it. The warmth seeped through the fabric and into her skin, not unpleasant but strange, as if she were holding a living coal that did not burn. She moved slowly through the cave passage, turning sideways to squeeze through the narrow entrance, and emerged blinking into the cold mountain air with the egg clutched tight against her body. The descent was treacherous, the muddy path even more dangerous with her arms occupied and her balance compromised, and twice she had to stop and brace herself against a rock to keep from sliding downhill. But she made it to the tree line without falling, and the forest rose up around her, dark and silent and welcoming in its concealment.

She found the shelter as the sun was beginning its descent toward the sea. It was exactly as her grandmother had described, a low stone structure built into a hillside, its roof made of slabs that had been fitted together with a precision that spoke of careful hands and patient work. Moss covered most of the exterior, and a young pine had grown up beside the entrance, its branches drooping low enough to hide the doorway from anyone who was not looking for it. Lina pushed through the branches and ducked inside, and the interior was dry and surprisingly warm, sheltered from the wind by thick stone walls and heated by the earth itself. A fire pit sat in the center of the floor, ringed with blackened stones, and a hole in the roof above it would carry smoke up and away. Someone had used this place before, and recently enough that the fire pit still held the grey remnants of old ash.

She settled the egg in a corner where the wall met the floor, arranging her cloak around it to cushion the stone, and then she sat back and watched the light pulse in the dim interior of the shelter. The journey had tired her more than she had expected, and her arms ached from carrying the weight, but there was satisfaction in seeing the egg here, in this hidden place, safe from hunters and storms and the eyes of anyone who might wish it harm. She ate the bread and fish she had packed, drank from her waterskin, and allowed herself a moment of rest before she would have to begin the walk back to the village. Her mother would be wondering where she was. The pinecones she was supposed to be gathering did not exist. Another lie would be required, another deception added to the growing weight of secrets she was learning to carry.

The sound came without warning, a sharp crack that echoed off the stone walls and made Lina's heart leap into her throat. She scrambled to her feet and turned toward the egg, and what she saw stopped her breath entirely. A line had appeared across the shell, dark against the pulsing gold, and as she watched another crack split the surface, and another, spreading outward in a web of fractures that glowed from within. The egg was hatching. The egg was hatching now, here, while she watched, and Lina did not know what to do or where to go or how to help. She stood frozen as the cracks widened, as pieces of shell began to fall away, as the light inside grew brighter until she had to shield her eyes against the glare.

Then the light faded, and the shell fell apart, and something moved in the pile of fragments and ash that remained.

The dragon was smaller than she had expected, no bigger than a cat, its body covered in scales the color of cooling ash. Its wings were folded tight against its sides, damp and crumpled, and its eyes were closed, its head tucked against its chest as if it were still sleeping. For a long moment it did not move, and Lina felt a terrible fear grip her heart, a fear that she had done something wrong, that the journey had harmed it, that the creature had died in the very act of being born. But then its head lifted, and its eyes opened, and Lina found herself looking into depths of amber that seemed to hold all the fire of the world within them.

The dragon looked at her. She looked back. Neither of them moved. The shelter was silent except for the soft sound of the dragon's breathing, quick and shallow, and the distant whisper of wind in the pines outside. Lina did not know what to do. She did not know what dragons expected from the first creature they saw, did not know if this small ash-colored thing would see her as a threat or a mother or something else entirely. She only knew that she could not look away, could not break the connection that had formed between her eyes and those amber depths, and that something inside her chest was responding to the dragon's gaze with a warmth that had nothing to do with fire.

"Hello," she said, and her voice came out as barely more than a whisper. The dragon's head tilted, its eyes tracking the movement of her lips, and it made a sound, a soft chirping noise that seemed to come from deep in its throat. Lina felt herself smile despite everything, despite the fear and the uncertainty and the knowledge of what she had done. The dragon chirped again, and this time its wings unfolded slightly, stretching and testing the air as if remembering how they were supposed to work. Its scales caught the dim light filtering through the smoke hole, and Lina could see now that they were not uniformly grey but shot through with veins of darker color, charcoal and black that traced patterns across its small body.

She lowered herself slowly to the ground, moving carefully to avoid startling the creature, and extended one hand toward it the way she had seen Finn extend his hand toward the dragon on the cliff. The dragon watched her approach, its amber eyes unblinking, and Lina held her breath as her fingers drew closer to its snout. The scales were warm beneath her touch, warmer than the egg had been, and smooth except for the raised ridges where the darker colors ran. The dragon pressed its head into her palm, and that chirping sound came again, and Lina felt something shift inside her, some barrier she had not known existed crumbling away to reveal a connection she could not name but could not deny.

"You understand me," she said, and it was not a question. The dragon chirped once more and stepped closer, its small claws clicking against the stone floor, its wings spreading wider now as they dried in the shelter's warmth. It was looking at her with an intensity that made her feel seen in a way she had never been seen before, not by her mother or the villagers or anyone she had ever known. This creature, this forbidden thing that should not exist, was looking at her as if she mattered. As if she was not just a quiet girl who gathered driftwood and told lies and tried not to be noticed. As if she was something more.

"I don't know how to take care of you," she admitted, and the words felt dangerous, an acknowledgment of everything she did not know and could not do. "I don't know what you eat or where you should sleep or how to keep you hidden from people who want to hurt you. I don't know anything about dragons except that everyone says they're dangerous and need to be destroyed." She paused, her hand still resting on the dragon's warm scales. "But I don't believe that anymore. I saw one of your kind on the cliff, and it wasn't dangerous. It was just alive. It just wanted to live." The dragon pressed closer, its body curling against her knee, and Lina felt her eyes sting with tears she did not fully understand. "I'm going to try," she said. "I'm going to try to keep you safe. I don't know if I can do it, but I'm going to try."

The dragon made a new sound, lower than the chirp, a soft rumbling that Lina felt as much as heard. It vibrated through the scales beneath her hand, through the stone beneath her knees, through the air itself, and she recognized it from the cliff, from the moment when Finn's hand had touched the larger dragon's snout. Trust. The sound meant trust. She did not know how she knew this, but she knew it as surely as she knew her own name, and the knowledge filled her with a warmth that pushed back against the cold fear that had been living in her chest since she first found the egg.

The sun was setting by the time she left the shelter, painting the sky above the forest canopy in shades of orange and red that reminded her of dragon fire. The creature was sleeping now, curled in the nest she had made from her cloak, its breathing slow and steady, its small body rising and falling with each breath. She had gathered what kindling she could find and built a small fire in the pit, just enough to keep the shelter warm through the night, and she had promised the dragon she would return tomorrow with food, though she did not know yet what dragons ate.

The walk home would be long and dark, and her mother would be worried, and there would be questions she could not answer honestly. But none of that seemed to matter as much as it should. Something had changed in that shelter, in that moment when amber eyes met hers and a connection formed that she could not explain.

She had a dragon now. A small, ash-grey dragon that trusted her, that responded to her voice and her touch, that had chosen to press its head into her palm instead of fleeing or fighting. The weight of that responsibility settled onto her shoulders, heavier than the egg had been, heavier than any burden she had carried before. But beneath the weight there was something else, something that felt almost like purpose. She was not just a quiet girl anymore. She was a keeper of secrets, a protector of forbidden things, a carrier of fire that burned unseen.

The forest closed around her as she walked, dark and silent, and Lina did not look back.

CHAPTER 3

SMALL FLAMES

Lina crouched at the mouth of the stone shelter, watching Spark nose the pile of fish she had stolen from the drying racks before dawn. The little dragon sniffed once, twice, then turned away and pressed herself into the far corner of the ruin, her ash-grey scales catching what little light filtered through the gaps in the collapsed roof.

Three days. Three days since the egg had cracked open before her, since that first moment when amber eyes had blinked up at her and something had shifted in her chest like a door swinging wide. Three days of sneaking out before her mother woke, of lying about where she had been, of watching Spark grow weaker instead of stronger.

"You have to eat," Lina whispered. "Please."

Spark lifted her head. Her wings, still too large for her body, folded tighter against her sides. A thin curl of smoke rose from her nostrils—not the bright, eager flame Lina had seen on that first night, but something weaker. Uncertain.

Lina pressed her palms against her knees. She did not know what she was doing. She had never raised anything larger than a chicken, and chickens did not breathe fire or watch you with eyes that seemed to hold questions you could not answer.

"I'm sorry," she said, though she was not sure what she was apologizing for. For not knowing how to help. For hiding Spark here instead of somewhere better. For being the only person standing between this creature and a kingdom that wanted it dead.

Spark made a sound—low and rough, somewhere between a growl and a whimper. The smoke from her nostrils thinned to nothing.

Lina sat back on her heels and studied the fish. They were fresh enough. She had checked them herself, had pressed her thumb into the flesh the way her mother had taught her. Nothing wrong with them.

So why wouldn't Spark eat?

The forest path back to the village wound between pines so tall their tops disappeared into the grey morning sky. Lina walked quickly, her boots crunching over frozen needles, her mind circling the same problem over and over.

Dragons were hunters. Everyone knew that. They ate fish, goats, deer—anything they could catch. The old songs said they had once helped clear the frozen sea paths, diving beneath the ice to drive schools of fish toward human nets. They were not supposed to refuse food and press themselves into corners and watch you with eyes full of something that looked almost like grief.

But then, Lina thought, the old songs also said dragons chose their companions. That they bonded through trust, not force.

That they could sense what a person felt before words were ever spoken.

She stopped in the middle of the path.

Sense what a person felt.

Lina pressed her hand to her chest, where her heart beat too fast beneath her ribs. Every time she entered that shelter, she was afraid. Afraid of being caught, afraid of failing, afraid of watching Spark grow weaker until the little dragon simply stopped breathing. She had been carrying that fear with her like a stone in her pocket, and Spark—

Spark had felt every bit of it.

"Oh," Lina breathed. The word hung in the cold air, a small cloud of white.

Dragons were not wild beasts to be fed and contained. They were emotional. They responded to the people around them, mirrored fear with fear, calm with trust. Everything Lina had been feeling—the panic, the doubt, the constant sense that she was doing everything wrong—Spark had absorbed it all.

No wonder the dragon would not eat. She was too afraid to be hungry.

The village was already awake when Lina reached the edge of the tree line. Smoke rose from the longhouses, thin grey threads against the pale sky. She could hear the distant clang of the blacksmith's hammer, the shouts of fishermen hauling their boats down to the water.

And voices. Too many voices gathered near the center square.

Lina slowed her steps. A crowd had formed near the elder's hall—a proper crowd, the kind that only gathered when travelers arrived or when someone had died. She moved closer, keeping to the edges, until she could see what had drawn everyone's attention.

A man stood on the hall's steps. He wore the king's colors—black and iron-grey—and his voice carried across the square like a hammer striking stone.

"Reports of dragon activity in the eastern reaches. His Majesty has ordered increased patrols. Anyone with information about dragon sightings, nesting sites, or those who aid these creatures will be rewarded."

Lina's hands went cold.

"Conversely," the man continued, "anyone found harboring dragons or protecting their eggs will face the full weight of the king's justice."

The crowd murmured. Lina saw her neighbor, old Marta, cross her arms over her chest. Saw young Torvin lean close to his brother and whisper something that made them both look toward the forest.

Toward the forest where Spark was hidden.

"The hunts will resume within the fortnight," the king's man said. "Any able-bodied person who wishes to join may present themselves at the garrison. The crown provides weapons and pays well."

He said more after that, but Lina did not hear it. Blood rushed in her ears, drowning everything else. Dragon hunts. Patrols. Rewards for information.

She thought of Spark pressing herself into the corner of that ruined shelter, smoke dying in her nostrils, eyes full of fear that was not her own.

Lina turned and walked back toward the forest. She did not run—running would draw attention—but her steps were quick and her breath came short, and by the time she reached the shelter her hands were shaking.

Spark had not moved.

The little dragon was still curled in the corner, her wings wrapped tight around her body, her tail tucked beneath her chin. She looked up when Lina entered, and something in her amber eyes flickered. Recognition, maybe, or hope.

Lina stood very still. She thought about the king's man in the village square, about the hunts that would come, about everything she risked by being here. The fear was still there, coiled tight beneath her ribs. She could not make it disappear.

But she could choose what to do with it.

Lina lowered herself to the ground. Not crouching this time—sitting, properly, with her back against the stone wall and her legs stretched out in front of her. She took a breath. Let it out slowly.

"I'm scared," she said quietly. "I don't know what I'm doing. I've never taken care of anything like you before, and there are people looking for dragons now, and I'm terrified that I'm going to fail you."

Spark's head lifted slightly.

"But I'm not going to leave," Lina continued. "I found you. I chose to bring you here. And I'm going to figure this out, even if I don't know how yet."

She let the words settle into the silence. The fear was still there, but it felt different now—acknowledged instead of hidden, carried instead of buried. She thought about the old songs again, about dragons sensing intent before words were spoken.

Maybe it was not about being fearless. Maybe it was about being honest.

Spark uncurled slowly. Her wings loosened from her body. She took one step toward Lina, then another, her claws clicking softly against the stone floor.

Lina held very still. She did not reach out. Did not try to coax or encourage. She simply sat and waited, letting Spark make her own choice.

The dragon crossed the remaining distance and pressed her head against Lina's knee.

The touch sent a warmth through Lina's chest—not heat, not fire, but something gentler. A settling. Recognition. She lifted her hand slowly and rested it on Spark's neck, feeling the pulse beneath the scales, the warmth that no longer felt dangerous.

"There you are," Lina whispered.

Spark made a sound, low and rumbling, and a small flame flickered in her throat—steady this time, not wild. Calm.

Lina reached for the pile of fish without looking away from Spark's eyes. She picked one up and held it out, palm flat, the way she had once offered apples to the village horses.

Spark sniffed it. Hesitated.

"It's all right," Lina said. "We're all right."

The dragon took the fish.

By the time the sun had climbed to its midday height, Spark had eaten three fish and was working on a fourth. She ate messily, tearing chunks with teeth that were sharper than Lina had realized, scales around her mouth slick with oil. It should have been disgusting. Instead, Lina found herself smiling.

"Slow down," she murmured. "You'll make yourself sick."

Spark ignored her and kept eating. Her wings had relaxed now, spread slightly at her sides, and the tension had drained from her body. She looked like a different creature than the one Lina had found curled in the corner that morning—still small, still young, but no longer shrinking.

Lina leaned back against the wall and watched. The fear was still there, waiting at the edges of her thoughts—the king's man, the hunts, everything that could go wrong. But it no longer felt like drowning. It felt like something she could hold.

She thought about what she knew. Dragons were emotional. They responded to calm with trust. They needed to feel safe before they could do anything else.

That meant the hiding place was important. The shelter was far from the village, but it was exposed. Anyone could stumble upon it—a hunter tracking deer, a child exploring the forest, a patrol sweeping the area for exactly what Lina was trying to protect.

She needed somewhere better. Somewhere deeper in the woods, or higher in the hills, where the king's men were less likely to search. Somewhere Spark could grow without the constant pressure of discovery.

"I'll find it," Lina said quietly. "I'll figure something out."

Spark looked up from her fish. Her amber eyes caught Lina's and held them, and for a moment Lina could have sworn she understood. Not the words, maybe, but the intent behind them. The promise.

The dragon returned to her meal. Lina stayed where she was, back against the cold stone, hand resting on her knee where Spark had pressed her head.

She did not know how to train a dragon. She did not know how to keep either of them safe. She did not know anything except that leaving was not an option, that giving up was not something she could do.

Maybe that was enough. Maybe it had to be.

Outside the shelter, wind moved through the pines. Somewhere in the distance, a bird called—sharp and clear, cutting through the winter silence. Lina listened to it and thought about the village, about the king's man standing on the steps of the elder's hall, about rumors spreading like fire through dry grass.

The hunts were coming.

But for now, in this moment, she had a dragon who trusted her enough to eat from her hand.

For now, that would have to be enough.

Spark finished the last fish and curled up against Lina's side. Her scales were warm—not burning, just warm, like stones that had been sitting in the sun. Her breathing slowed, deepened. Within moments, she was asleep.

Lina did not move. She sat in the quiet shelter, one hand resting on Spark's neck, and let herself believe, for just a little while, that caring was enough. That this was something she could do. That they would find a way.

TRACKS IN THE ASHES

Two hundred and fourteen steps from the edge of the village to the first marker. It was a split pine struck by lightning years before she was born. Another eighty-six to the stream crossing, where flat stones made a path through the shallow water. Then three hundred and forty through the densest part of the Pinewild, where the trees grew so close their branches wove together overhead and blocked out the sky.

She walked the route twice a day now. Once before dawn, when her mother still slept and the village was quiet. Once in the failing light of evening, when shadows stretched long and anyone watching might mistake her for just another girl gathering kindling.

It had been a week since the king's messenger came. A week of careful steps and held breath and the constant, gnawing fear that today would be the day someone followed her into the trees.

But no one had. The village went about its business—fishing, mending nets, preparing for the winter that crept closer each day. The messenger's words had stirred whispers for a day or two, then faded into the background noise of ordinary life.

Lina allowed herself to hope. Perhaps the danger had passed. Perhaps the hunts would focus elsewhere—on the eastern reaches the messenger had mentioned, far from this small village beneath the cliffs. Perhaps she and Spark could remain hidden until—

Until what?

She pushed the thought away as she reached the shelter. The stone walls rose before her, half-collapsed but solid enough to keep out the wind. Inside, Spark lifted her head at the sound of Lina's footsteps.

The dragon had grown. Not much—it had only been a week—but enough that Lina noticed. Her wings seemed less awkward now, folding properly against her sides instead of jutting at odd angles. Her scales had darkened from pale ash to something closer to charcoal, with hints of copper beneath when the light caught them right.

"I brought fish," Lina said, kneeling to empty her satchel. "And something else."

She pulled out a bundle wrapped in cloth—scraps of dried meat she had taken from the smokehouse when no one was looking. It was a risk, stealing from the village stores, but Spark needed more than fish. Lina had watched her growing restless, pacing the confines of the shelter, and knew instinctively that variety mattered.

Spark sniffed the meat and made a sound low in her throat. Approval, Lina thought. Or at least interest.

"You need to stay inside today," Lina said as the dragon began to eat. "I saw hunters on the cliff path this morning. They weren't looking for dragons—just deer, I think—but they're too close."

Spark paused mid-bite. Her amber eyes found Lina's face.

"I know," Lina said quietly. "I know you want to go outside. But not yet. Not until they move on."

The dragon returned to her meal, but something in the set of her wings told Lina she understood. Dragons sensed intent, not words—but intent was enough.

The problem came that afternoon.

Lina was halfway home when she smelled it. Smoke—not the clean smoke of a cooking fire, but something sharper. Wilder. She stopped on the path, heart suddenly loud in her chest, and turned to look back the way she had come.

A thin column of grey rose above the treetops. It came from the direction of the shelter.

Lina ran.

The forest blurred around her—pine needles underfoot, branches slapping at her arms, her own breath harsh in her ears. She did not count her steps. She did not think about being seen. She thought only of Spark, of that thin ribbon of smoke rising where no smoke should be, of everything she had risked and everything she stood to lose.

The shelter came into view. The smoke was coming from inside—seeping through the gaps in the roof, curling around the edges of the doorway. Lina burst through the entrance and found

Spark pressed against the far wall, wings half-spread, small flames licking from her nostrils with each panicked breath.

A pile of dry leaves in the corner was burning. Not much—the flames had only just caught—but enough to send smoke spiraling upward.

"No, no, no," Lina said. She grabbed her cloak and smothered the fire, pressing the heavy wool down until the flames died and only embers remained. Smoke stung her eyes. She blinked rapidly and turned to Spark.

The dragon was trembling.

"It's all right," Lina said, though her voice shook. "It's all right. It was an accident."

Spark made a sound—a low, rough whine that Lina recognized as distress. The flames in her nostrils flickered and died. She pressed her head against Lina's hand, scales warm with what felt like shame.

"You didn't mean to," Lina murmured, stroking the ridge above Spark's eyes. "I know. Fire reflects emotion—that's what you were trying to tell me, wasn't it? Something scared you."

Spark's eyes darted toward the entrance.

Lina went cold. "Someone was here?"

A sound came from outside. Footsteps. Careful, measured footsteps moving through the underbrush.

Lina's hand tightened on Spark's neck. "Hide," she whispered. "Behind the stones. Don't make a sound."

The dragon hesitated, eyes wide with fear that was not her own—fear she was absorbing from Lina, mirroring back in the tension of her body and the smoke that threatened to rise again from her throat.

"Please," Lina breathed. "Trust me."

Spark moved. She pressed herself into the deepest shadows of the ruined shelter, behind a tumble of fallen stones, her dark scales blending with the darkness until she was nearly invisible.

Lina grabbed her cloak—still warm from smothering the fire—and stepped outside.

A boy stood at the edge of the clearing.

Lina recognized him immediately. Finn—the boy she had watched from the cliffs what felt like a lifetime ago. He stood with his weight balanced, ready to move in any direction, his light hair catching the afternoon sun. His eyes were fixed on her face.

"There was smoke," he said. His voice was calm, but Lina saw him scan the shelter behind her, then the trees, then back to her. Checking for danger. "I've been tracking it for three days."

Three days. Lina's stomach dropped. She thought she had been careful. She thought she had hidden every trace.

"Smoke from what?" she asked, and was surprised at how steady her voice sounded.

Finn's eyes narrowed slightly. "That's what I've been trying to figure out. Small fires, appearing and disappearing. No campsites. No cooking pits. Just—" He paused, and something shifted in his expression. "Just heat. In places where heat shouldn't be."

Lina forced herself not to look back at the shelter. "Maybe lightning. There was a storm last week."

"Lightning doesn't leave ash in patterns," Finn said quietly. "And it doesn't move."

The silence stretched between them. Lina could feel Spark behind her, hidden in the darkness, and she knew—knew with absolute certainty—that if Finn took three more steps toward the shelter, he would see her. The stones were not enough cover. The shadows were not deep enough. One wrong move, one moment of panic, and everything would be over.

"I'm gathering kindling," Lina said. "My mother sent me. The shelter's been abandoned for years—I use it to store what I find."

Finn studied her. His gaze was direct, assessing, and she had the uncomfortable feeling that he was reading her the way he might read tracks in the snow. Looking for signs. Looking for what didn't fit.

"You're the girl from the village," he said. "I've seen you on the cliff path."

"Lina," she said, because lying about her name seemed pointless.

"Finn." He glanced past her at the shelter again, and Lina's heart stopped. Then he looked back at her face. "The smoke today. It came from in there."

Not a question. A statement.

Lina's mind raced. She could lie again—claim she had been burning brush, clearing the shelter of debris. But Finn had been tracking fires for three days. He knew something was wrong. A simple lie would not satisfy him.

"I burned some old leaves," she said carefully. "They were damp. I didn't realize they would smoke so much."

Finn was quiet for a long moment. Then he took a breath—slow, deliberate, the kind of breath someone takes when they are deciding whether to push further or let something go.

"Be more careful," he said finally. "The king's hunters are in the region. They're looking for signs of dragons, and smoke draws attention."

The words hung in the air. Lina searched his face for accusation, for the sharp edge of suspicion, but found only something that might have been warning.

"I will," she managed.

Finn nodded once. He looked at the shelter one last time—long enough that Lina stopped breathing—and then he turned and walked back into the forest.

Lina did not move until his footsteps faded. Then she sagged against the shelter's doorframe, her legs suddenly weak, her hands shaking so badly she had to press them flat against the stone.

Inside, Spark emerged from her hiding place.

The dragon pressed her warm scales against Lina's side and made a sound that was almost questioning. Lina sank down beside her and wrapped her arms around Spark's neck, breathing in the strange, smoky scent that clung to her scales.

"That was too close," she whispered. "That was so much too close."

Spark rumbled softly. Her flame had settled—no more wild flickers, no more panic-smoke. But Lina could feel the tension in her body, the wariness that had not fully faded.

Three days. Finn had been tracking them for three days, and Lina had not even known. She had walked her careful route, counted her steps, believed that caution was enough—and all the while, someone had been watching the signs she left behind.

Lina thought about the way Finn had looked at the shelter. The way he had said *be more careful*, like a warning instead of a threat.

He knew. He had to know. No one tracked fires for three days without understanding what they were tracking.

But he had walked away.

Why?

Lina pressed her face against Spark's neck and tried to think. The hunters were in the region—Finn had said so himself. If he told them what he suspected, they would come. They would search the forest with nets and chains and whatever other tools the king used to capture dragons. They would find Spark, and then—

She could not finish the thought.

"We need to move," she said against Spark's scales. "Tonight. Somewhere deeper in the forest, or higher in the hills. Somewhere no one will think to look."

Spark shifted. Her wings rustled—not in fear this time, but something else. Readiness, maybe. Trust.

Lina lifted her head. The light was already fading, shadows lengthening across the shelter floor. She had maybe an hour before full dark, and she did not know this forest well enough to navigate it at night.

Tomorrow, then. She would scout a new location tomorrow, find somewhere safer, move Spark before anyone else could track them.

But even as she made the plan, she knew the truth.

Secrecy was not working.

She had believed that hiding was enough—that if she was careful, if she covered her tracks, if she kept Spark contained, no one would ever know. But Finn had found the signs she did not even realize she was leaving. And if he could find them, others could too.

The king's hunters. The soldiers. Anyone with eyes sharp enough to see what should not be there.

Lina's throat tightened. She had wanted to believe they were safe. She needed to believe it, because the alternative was too frightening to face.

But fear was not protection. And believing a thing did not make it true.

"I'm sorry," she whispered to Spark. "I thought I could keep us hidden. I thought if I was just careful enough—"

She did not finish. There was nothing to finish. Careful had not been enough, and now she did not know what would be.

Spark pressed her head against Lina's shoulder. The warmth was steady now, comforting in a way that felt like forgiveness.

Outside, the wind picked up, moving through the pines with a sound like distant voices. Lina listened to it and thought about Finn walking away through the trees, about the warning he had given her, about all the questions she could not answer.

He knew. She was almost certain now.

And she had no idea what he would do with that knowledge.

The fear that had settled in her chest since the king's messenger came was no longer quiet. It pressed against her ribs, made her breath come short, whispered all the ways this could end badly. She had thought she understood fear—had learned to acknowledge it, to carry it instead of hiding from it.

But this was different. This was the fear of being hunted, of knowing someone was watching, of realizing that every step she took left marks she could not see.

Lina held Spark closer and waited for the dark.

Tomorrow, she would find a new hiding place. Tomorrow, she would be smarter, more careful, better at covering her tracks.

But tonight, all she could do was sit with the weight of what she now understood: that she was not invisible, that her secret had edges others could find, and that somewhere in the darkening forest, a boy who knew about dragons had seen enough to guess the truth.

The question was not whether he knew.

The question was what he would do next.

CHAPTER 5

THE BOY IN THE PINES

Lina lay in her narrow bed, listening to her mother's breathing in the next room, and stared at the wooden beams above her head. Every time she closed her eyes, she saw Finn standing at the edge of the clearing. The way he had looked at the shelter. The way he had said *be more careful*, like he already knew what she was hiding.

By the time grey light crept through the shutters, she had decided. She could not keep doing this alone.

The thought felt like failure. She had promised herself she would protect Spark, had believed that if she was just careful enough, quiet enough, invisible enough, no one would ever have to know. But Finn had found her anyway. He had tracked her signs for three days, and she had not even realized she was leaving them.

forest, a boy who knew about dragons had seen enough to guess the truth.

The question was not whether he knew.

The question was what he would do next.

CHAPTER 5

THE BOY IN THE PINES

Lina lay in her narrow bed, listening to her mother's breathing in the next room, and stared at the wooden beams above her head. Every time she closed her eyes, she saw Finn standing at the edge of the clearing. The way he had looked at the shelter. The way he had said *be more careful*, like he already knew what she was hiding.

By the time grey light crept through the shutters, she had decided. She could not keep doing this alone.

The thought felt like failure. She had promised herself she would protect Spark, had believed that if she was just careful enough, quiet enough, invisible enough, no one would ever have to know. But Finn had found her anyway. He had tracked her signs for three days, and she had not even realized she was leaving them.

She was not good enough at this. She did not know enough. And if she kept trying to do it alone, she would make a mistake that could not be undone.

Lina slipped out of bed before her mother woke. She moved through the village in the thin morning light, past the longhouses with their banked fires, past the drying racks heavy with fish, past the paths she had walked a thousand times before. But instead of turning toward the Pinewild, she climbed.

The cliffs rose behind the village like the spine of some great beast. Lina had come here as a child to watch the sea, to feel the wind pull at her hair and imagine she was somewhere else, someone else. Now she climbed with purpose, following the narrow path that wound upward through the rocks.

She found what she was looking for near the top: a flat ledge where the path widened, sheltered from the wind by an outcropping of stone. Scorch marks darkened the rock in places. Old marks, faded by weather and time, but still visible if you knew what to look for.

This was where she had first seen Finn with a dragon. This was where it had started.

Lina sat down on the cold stone and waited.

He came an hour after dawn.

Lina heard his footsteps before she saw him—steady, unhurried, the deliberate pace of someone who had learned to move without startling the creatures he worked with. He rounded the outcropping and stopped when he saw her sitting there.

For a long moment, neither of them spoke.

"You came back," Finn said finally. His voice was neutral, careful. "I wasn't sure you would."

"You knew I would be here?"

"I hoped." He moved closer, stopping a few paces away. His eyes swept over her face, reading her the way he had yesterday, looking for signs. "You looked like someone who needed to talk. And this is where people come when they need to think."

Lina's hands tightened in her lap. She had rehearsed this conversation a dozen times during the sleepless night, but now that the moment was here, all her careful words had fled.

"You know," she said. It was not a question.

Finn was quiet for a breath. Two. Then he lowered himself to the stone across from her, sitting with his back against the cliff face and his legs stretched out in front of him.

"I know there's a dragon in that shelter," he said. "I've known since the second day I tracked the fire signs. The patterns were too consistent to be anything else."

Lina's chest tightened. "Why didn't you tell anyone?"

"Because I wanted to see who was protecting it first." Finn's gaze held hers, steady and unreadable. "Dragon hunters don't hide their kills. They display them. You were covering tracks. Smothering fires. Trying to keep something alive instead of proving something dead."

The words hung in the cold air between them. Lina searched his face for judgment, for the anger she had expected, but found only that same careful watchfulness.

"You're not going to turn me in," she said slowly.

"No."

"Why?"

Finn looked away, toward the sea stretching grey and endless below them. When he spoke, his voice was quieter than before.

"Because I've spent three years learning everything I could about dragons. How they think. How they feel. How to earn their trust instead of forcing their obedience." He paused. "And in all that time, I've never seen what you have."

Lina frowned. "What do you mean?"

"A wild hatchling," Finn said, turning back to face her. "A dragon that chose you. Do you understand how rare that is? Dragons don't bond with just anyone. They sense intent. They read emotion. And they only trust humans who have—" He stopped, searching for the right word. "Who have a certain kind of fire in them."

"I don't have fire," Lina said. "I'm not brave. I'm not special. I just found an egg and didn't want it to die."

"That's exactly what I mean." Finn leaned forward slightly. "You didn't approach that egg thinking about what you could gain. You weren't trying to prove anything or claim anything. You just wanted to protect it."

"Anyone would have done the same."

"No." The word was flat, certain. "They wouldn't. Most people would have left it there. Or smashed it. Or run to tell someone who would do the smashing for them." Finn's eyes were intense now, that careful neutrality stripped away. "You chose to save it. And then you chose to keep saving it, day after day, even when you didn't know what you were doing. That's what dragons respond to. Not skill. Not knowledge. Choice."

Lina stared at him. She thought about the old songs, the ones that said dragons bonded through trust, not force. She thought about Spark pressing her head against her knee, about the warmth that spread through her chest when they were together, about the way the dragon seemed to know what she was feeling before she felt it herself.

"I don't understand," she said quietly. "I don't know anything about dragons. I've been making it up as I go."

"I know." A ghost of something crossed Finn's face—not quite a smile, but close. "That's why I came back yesterday. I had to see for myself."

"See what?"

"If the bond was real." He paused. "It is. I could tell from the fire patterns. A dragon's flame reflects emotion—did you know that? Steady when they're calm, wild when they're afraid. The fires I tracked were small and controlled. That doesn't happen with wild dragons. It only happens when they feel safe."

Lina remembered Spark's flame flickering in her throat—steady, warm, nothing like the panicked fire that had started when she was frightened. She had thought she understood what that meant, but hearing Finn explain it made it feel more real. More significant.

"She trusts me," Lina said.

"She does. And that's—" Finn stopped, took a breath. When he continued, his voice was rough. "That's something I've been trying to earn for three years and never quite managed."

They walked to the shelter together.

Lina had expected to feel afraid, leading someone else to Spark's hiding place. But the fear that had lived in her chest since the king's messenger came felt different now. Smaller. Shared.

She's not alone.

The thought surprised her with its force. She had been carrying this secret for weeks, convinced that telling anyone would mean disaster. But Finn already knew. He had known for days. And instead of turning her in, he was walking beside her through the Pinewild, asking questions about how she had found the egg and what she had fed Spark and whether the dragon had started trying to fly yet.

"She stretches her wings sometimes," Lina said. "But she hasn't tried to leave the shelter."

"She's probably waiting."

"For what?"

"For you to tell her it's safe." Finn ducked under a low branch. "Dragons are cautious when they're young. They rely on their bonded human to read the world for them, to know when it's all right to move and when it's better to stay hidden."

Lina thought about all the times she had told Spark to stay inside, to keep quiet, to wait. She had thought she was protecting the dragon. But maybe she had also been holding her back.

"How do you know all this?" she asked.

Finn was quiet for several steps. When he spoke, his voice was careful again, measured.

"There was an elder in my village. She remembered the old ways—how dragons and humans used to live together, before the king's purge. She taught me what she knew." A pause. "She's gone now. Disappeared two winters ago. But the knowledge didn't disappear with her."

Lina heard the grief beneath the words, carefully contained but present. "I'm sorry."

"Don't be. She made her choice." Finn's jaw tightened. "The hunters were getting too close. She led them away from the dragons she was protecting. I don't know if she's dead or just hiding somewhere they can't find her. But I know she'd rather be gone than let them win."

They reached the shelter. Lina paused at the entrance, suddenly uncertain. Spark had never seen anyone except her. What if the dragon panicked? What if she breathed fire, or tried to hide, or refused to come out at all?

"It's all right," Finn said quietly. He had stopped a few paces back, giving her space. "I'll wait here. Let her see you first."

Lina nodded and stepped inside.

Spark was awake.

The dragon stood in the center of the shelter, her head turned toward the entrance, her amber eyes fixed on the doorway. She had known someone was coming—had probably sensed Finn's presence long before Lina heard his footsteps.

"It's all right," Lina said softly. She crossed to Spark and knelt beside her, one hand resting on the dragon's neck. "He's not a hunter. He's—" She paused, searching for the right word. "He's like me. He wants to help."

Spark's scales were warm under her palm—not hot, not panicked, but that steady warmth Lina had come to recognize as trust. The dragon's eyes stayed fixed on the doorway, but her body was relaxed, her wings folded calmly at her sides.

She's reading me, Lina realized. *She knows I'm not afraid, so she's not afraid either.*

"Finn," she called. "You can come in."

He entered slowly, each movement deliberate and unhurried. He stopped just inside the entrance and stood very still, his hands visible at his sides, his posture open and unthreatening.

Spark watched him. A thin curl of smoke rose from her nostrils—not flame, just smoke, the dragon equivalent of wariness.

"Hello," Finn said quietly. His voice was different than Lina had heard before—almost reverent. "It's been a long time since I've seen an Emberwing this young."

"Emberwing?" Lina asked.

"Her species. They're the most common dragons in Frostmark—or they were, before the purge." Finn's eyes moved over Spark's form, taking in her ash-grey scales, her oversized wings, the copper undertones that showed when she shifted. "She's healthy. Growing well. You've done better than you know."

Something loosened in Lina's chest. She had been so afraid of doing everything wrong, of failing Spark through ignorance and inexperience. Hearing that she had done something right felt like the first full breath she had taken in weeks.

"She needs to fly," Finn continued. "Soon. Emberwings develop their fire control through flight—something about the way they use their wings to regulate heat. If she stays grounded too long, she'll have trouble controlling her flame."

"But the hunters—"

"I know." Finn's jaw tightened. "That's the problem. She needs to fly, but flying means being seen. And being seen means—" He didn't finish.

He didn't need to.

Spark made a sound—low, questioning—and took a step toward Finn. Lina felt her heart skip. The dragon had never approached anyone except her before.

Finn went very still. He did not reach out. Did not move at all. He simply waited, the way Lina had learned to wait, letting Spark make her own choice.

The dragon stopped a pace away from him. She stretched her neck forward and sniffed—once, twice—her nostrils flaring. Then she pulled back and returned to Lina's side, pressing against her leg.

"She's decided," Finn said quietly. There was something in his voice—not disappointment, exactly, but something close to it. "You're her person. She'll tolerate me, but she won't trust me the way she trusts you."

"Is that bad?"

"No." Finn met her eyes. "It's rare. It's what the old trainers used to call a Flame-Bind—a bond so strong it can't be broken or transferred. I've heard stories about it, but I've never seen it happen." He paused. "Until now."

Lina looked down at Spark, at the dragon who had chosen her, and felt the weight of that choice settle into her bones.

She had thought she was doing something wrong. She had believed, deep down, that someone else should be doing this—someone braver, stronger, more capable. Someone like Finn, who knew what he was doing, who had trained for years, who understood dragons in ways she never would.

But Spark had not chosen Finn. Spark had chosen her.

And maybe that meant something she did not fully understand yet.

They talked until the light began to fade.

Finn told her about the old ways—how dragons and humans had once lived in balance, helping each other survive the harsh winters of Frostmark. He explained how dragon fire had cleared sea paths of ice, how bonded pairs had defended villages from threats, how the relationship had been built on mutual choice rather than dominance or control.

"The king changed everything," he said. "He blamed dragons for a fire that destroyed part of the capital. Whether they actually caused it—" He shrugged. "No one knows. But he needed an enemy, and dragons were easier to hate than to understand."

"So he started hunting them."

"Worse than hunting. He made it a crime to help them. Anyone caught protecting a dragon, feeding one, even speaking in their defense—" Finn's voice hardened. "The punishment is death."

Lina's hand found Spark's neck, drawing comfort from the warmth beneath the scales. "But you help them anyway."

"Someone has to." Finn looked at her steadily. "And now there are two of us."

The words hung in the air. *Two of us.* Lina had come to the cliffs that morning believing she was alone, that no one could help her, that this burden was hers to carry and hers alone.

She had been wrong.

"I don't know what I'm doing," she said quietly. "I've been guessing. Getting lucky. But luck runs out."

"Then let me help you." Finn's voice was earnest now, the careful neutrality stripped away completely. "I can teach you what I know. How to read her moods, how to help her fly safely, how to hide the signs you don't even know you're leaving." He paused. "You have the bond. I have the knowledge. Together, we might actually keep her alive."

Lina looked at Spark. The dragon looked back, amber eyes steady, that small flame flickering in her throat—calm, trusting, waiting.

"Together," Lina said.

Finn nodded. Something shifted in his expression—relief, maybe, or something deeper.

"Tomorrow," he said. "We start tomorrow."

He rose and moved toward the entrance, then paused and looked back at her.

"You should know," he said quietly. "What you're doing—what you've already done—it's not nothing. You found an egg and chose to protect it. You raised a hatchling without any training, any guidance, any help. And you formed a Flame-Bind, which most people can't do even when they try." His eyes held hers. "You may think you're doing everything wrong, but Spark doesn't agree. And dragons don't lie."

He left before she could respond.

Lina sat in the shelter as darkness gathered outside, her hand resting on Spark's warm scales. The fear was still there—it would always be there, she understood now—but it felt different than before. Smaller. Manageable.

She was not alone anymore.

And maybe, just maybe, that was enough to make this impossible thing possible.

Spark pressed her head against Lina's shoulder and made a sound that was almost like a sigh. The flame in her throat flickered once, twice, then settled into something steady and warm.

Trust, Lina thought. *That's what it looks like.*

She leaned into the warmth and, for the first time in weeks, let herself believe they might actually survive this.

CHAPTER 6

WHAT THE ELDERS KNEW

F inn arrived at the shelter before dawn.

Lina was already there, sitting with her back against the stone wall and Spark curled beside her. She had not slept much—anticipation had kept her turning in her narrow bed—but she felt more awake than she had in weeks. Alert. Ready.

"You're early," Finn said, ducking through the entrance.

"So are you."

He almost smiled at that. Almost. Instead, he set down the leather satchel he carried and knelt to open it. Inside, Lina glimpsed coils of rope, strips of dried meat, and something wrapped in oilcloth.

"First lesson," Finn said. "Dragons learn through repetition and reward. Not punishment—never punishment. If you try to force a dragon, it will remember. And it will stop trusting you."

"I know," Lina said quietly. "I figured that out."

Finn paused, looking at her. "How?"

"She wouldn't eat. When I first brought her here." Lina's hand found Spark's neck, stroking the warm scales. "I was so afraid all the time—afraid of being caught, afraid of doing something wrong. And she felt it. She wouldn't eat because I was making her afraid."

"What did you do?"

"I told her the truth. That I was scared, but I wasn't going to leave." Lina shrugged, feeling the inadequacy of the words. "It sounds stupid when I say it out loud."

"It's not stupid." Finn's voice was serious. "It's exactly right. Dragons sense intent, not words. When you acknowledged your fear instead of hiding it, she understood that you weren't a threat. You were just—" He searched for the word. "Honest."

Spark lifted her head and made a soft sound, almost like agreement.

"The elder who taught me," Finn continued, "she used to say that dragons don't need us to be fearless. They need us to be true. Fear is natural. Pretending you don't have it—that's what breaks trust."

Lina thought about that. All her life, she had believed that courage meant not being afraid. That brave people were different from her, made of something stronger. But maybe that wasn't right. Maybe courage was just fear that kept moving forward anyway.

"What else did she teach you?" Lina asked.

Finn settled back on his heels, his expression shifting into something distant. "Everything I know. The old ways—how things were before the purge."

He told her about the Age of Dragons.

Three hundred years ago, Frostmark had been different. Dragons and humans lived in balance, each helping the other survive. Dragons cleared frozen sea paths with their fire, drove fish toward nets, protected villages from raiders and storms. In return, humans guarded nesting grounds, raised orphaned hatchlings, and honored the bond between species.

"It wasn't perfect," Finn said. "There were conflicts. Misunderstandings. Dragons are proud, and humans are—" He paused. "Humans are human. But it worked. For centuries, it worked."

"What changed?"

"Fear." The word was flat, hard. "A wildfire destroyed part of the capital. No one knows what really caused it. Maybe lightning, accident, something else entirely. But people were scared, and scared people need someone to blame."

"Dragons."

"Dragons." Finn nodded. "King Brann was young then, newly crowned, uncertain of his power. He saw an opportunity. If he could make people fear dragons more than they feared him, he could unite the kingdom against a common enemy."

Lina felt sick. "So he started hunting them."

"Worse than hunting. He made it a crime to help them. Eggs were destroyed on sight. Adults were captured and—" Finn's jaw tightened. "Killed publicly. Anyone who tried to protect them was declared a traitor. The punishment was death."

Spark pressed closer to Lina's side. The dragon's scales were warm, her breathing steady, but Lina could feel tension coiled beneath the surface. Even without understanding the words, Spark sensed the weight of them.

"And now?" Lina asked.

"Now most people think dragons are monsters. That's what the king wants them to believe. They've forgotten the old songs, the old stories. They've forgotten that fire doesn't have to destroy—it can also warm."

Finn reached into his satchel and pulled out the object wrapped in oilcloth. He unwrapped it carefully, revealing a stone the size of his palm. Its surface was dark, almost black, but when the light caught it, Lina saw faint lines etched into the surface—swirling patterns that might have been flames, or wings, or something older than either.

"What is that?"

"A hearthstone. From the old shrines." Finn turned it over in his hands. "The elder gave it to me before she disappeared. She said it was carved when dragons and humans still trusted each other—when the bond between them was something to celebrate, not hide."

He held it out to Lina. She took it, feeling the weight of it in her palm. The stone was warm—not hot, just warm, like it held some echo of the fires that had once burned in those forgotten shrines.

"Where is she now?" Lina asked. "The elder who taught you?"

Finn's expression shifted—a flicker of something raw crossing his face before he could hide it. He took the hearthstone back from her, turning it over in his hands like it was the only thing keeping him anchored.

"Gone," he said. "Two years now."

"Gone where?"

For a long moment, Finn didn't answer. Spark lifted her head, sensing the change in the air—the way grief could fill a space like smoke.

"Her name was Sera," Finn said finally. His voice was different now—quieter, younger somehow. "She found me when I was twelve. I was—" He paused, and Lina saw his jaw tighten. "I was trying to kill a dragon."

Lina stared at him. "What?"

"My father was a hunter. One of the king's best." Finn kept his eyes on the hearthstone. "He died when I was eleven. A dragon killed him—or that's what they told me. What they told everyone." He drew a slow breath. "I believed it. I was angry, and I wanted revenge, and when I heard rumors of a wounded Emberwing in the forests near my village, I went after it with my father's old crossbow."

Spark made a low sound—not quite a growl, but something wary. Lina put her hand on the dragon's neck, steadying her.

"What happened?"

"I found it. The Emberwing." Finn's voice was hollow. "It was dying. Caught in one of the king's traps, bleeding out, too weak to even lift its head. And I stood there with my crossbow aimed at its heart, ready to finish what the hunters had started."

He stopped. The silence stretched between them.

"But you didn't," Lina said softly.

"No." Finn finally looked up, and his eyes were wet. "Because it looked at me. This dying creature that should have been my enemy—it looked at me, and I saw... I don't know. Not rage. Not hatred. Just exhaustion. Just pain. And something else."

"What?"

"Recognition." Finn shook his head slowly. "Like it knew me. Like it understood that I was just a scared kid who had lost someone, and it was too tired to blame me for what I was about to do."

Lina's chest ached. She thought about Spark's egg in the cave, about the moment she had first felt that pull—the sense that this creature needed her, and maybe she needed it too.

"Sera found me standing there," Finn continued. "Crying over a dragon I'd come to kill. She didn't ask questions. She just knelt beside the Emberwing and started working—cleaning wounds, applying salves, talking to it in this low, calm voice." He paused. "It died anyway. Too much blood lost, too much damage. But she stayed with it until the end. And when it was over, she looked at me and said, 'Now you know.'"

"Know what?"

"That they're not monsters. That my father wasn't killed by a dragon—he was killed by fear. By a system that turns everyone into enemies." Finn's hand tightened on the hearthstone. "She told me the truth that night. That my father had been tracking a mother Emberwing who was just trying to protect her nest. That she fought back because he gave her no choice. That the 'monster' the king's hunters talked about was just a parent defending her children."

Lina felt tears prick her eyes. "Finn..."

"Sera took me in after that. Taught me everything she knew—the old ways, the training methods, the history that the king had tried to erase." His voice steadied slightly. "For five years, she was the only family I had. We saved eleven dragons together.

Found them homes in the wild places, helped them escape the hunts." He paused. "And then she heard about the prisoners at Ironhold."

The word hung in the air. Lina had not heard of Ironhold before, but the weight of it—the way Finn said it—told her everything she needed to know.

"She went after them," Lina said. It wasn't a question.

"She couldn't live with it. Knowing they were there, suffering, while she hid in the forests saving one dragon at a time." Finn's voice cracked slightly. "I begged her not to go. Told her it was suicide, that the king's fortress was impenetrable, that she'd be throwing her life away for nothing."

"What did she say?"

"She said that some things matter more than survival. That she'd rather die trying to free them than live knowing she hadn't tried." Finn finally met Lina's eyes, and she saw the grief there—old, deep, still raw. "She was right. I knew she was right. But I was scared, and I let her go alone."

"You were—how old? Seventeen?"

"Old enough to go with her. Old enough to fight." His jaw tightened. "But I didn't. I stayed behind, told myself I was being smart, being careful. And she never came back."

Spark moved then—not toward Lina, but toward Finn. The dragon crossed the space between them and pressed her snout gently against his shoulder. A gesture of comfort. Of understanding.

Finn's breath caught. He raised one hand slowly and rested it on Spark's scales.

"I don't know if she's dead," he said quietly. "The hunters never announced a capture. No public execution, no body. She just vanished." He stroked Spark's neck, and Lina saw his hand trembling. "For two years, I've been waiting. Hoping. Telling myself that maybe she escaped, maybe she's hiding somewhere, maybe someday she'll come back."

"Maybe she will."

"Maybe." But his voice said he didn't believe it. "Or maybe she died alone in that fortress, and I'll never know what happened to her. Because I was too afraid to go with her when she needed me."

Lina was quiet for a moment. She thought about all the times Finn had told her to be careful, to wait, to think before acting. She had assumed it was wisdom. Now she understood it was something else.

Guilt. The weight of a choice he couldn't take back.

"You were trying to survive," she said finally. "That's not nothing."

"Survival isn't enough." Finn pulled his hand back from Spark, but the dragon stayed close. "That's what Sera tried to tell me. That's what I've been learning, every day since she left. You can stay alive and still be dead inside. You can be safe and still lose everything that matters."

"Is that why you're helping me? Because of her?"

Finn considered the question. "Partly. When I saw you with Spark—the way you looked at her, the bond you'd formed without even trying—I saw what Sera always talked about. The old way. The real connection between dragons and humans." He paused. "But it's more than that."

"What do you mean?"

"You remind me of her." A ghost of a smile crossed his face. "Sera wasn't brave either—not the way people think of brave. She was just stubborn. Compassionate. Incapable of walking away from something that needed help." He looked at Lina. "You're the same. And maybe—if I can help you, teach you, keep you alive long enough to make a difference—maybe that's how I make up for not going with her."

Lina didn't know what to say. She had thought Finn was confident, capable, in control. But he was as broken as she was. Maybe more.

"You don't have to make up for anything," she said. "You were a kid. You were scared. That doesn't make you a coward—it makes you human."

"Maybe." Finn tucked the hearthstone back into his satchel. "But being human isn't an excuse. It's a reason to try harder." He looked at Spark, who had settled beside him like she belonged there. "Sera used to say that dragons forgive faster than humans. That they don't hold onto anger the way we do. They just—move forward."

Spark made a soft sound, and her flame flickered—warm, steady, accepting.

"Maybe we should learn from them," Lina said.

"Maybe we should." Finn stood, brushing dirt from his knees. When he looked at her again, some of the rawness had faded from his expression—replaced by something that might have been resolve. "That's why I'm showing you the hearthstone. That's why I'm telling you all of this."

"Why?"

"Because I want you to understand what we're protecting." Finn's eyes met hers. "It's not just Spark. It's not just one dragon. It's everything they represent. Balance. Choice. The idea that fire can warm instead of destroy."

Lina looked down at Spark, at the ancient patterns she imagined on unseen stones. She thought about Spark pressing her head against her knee, about the warmth that spread through her chest when they were together, about all the ways this small dragon had changed her without either of them meaning it to happen.

"I didn't mean for any of this," she said quietly. "I just found an egg. I just didn't want it to die."

"I know."

"I'm not brave, Finn. I'm not a hero from the old songs. I'm just—" She stopped, struggling to find the right words. "I'm just a girl who couldn't walk away."

"That's exactly what makes you different." Finn leaned forward slightly. "The old trainers—the ones who formed Flame-Binds—they weren't warriors. They weren't chosen by prophecy or born with special gifts. They were just people who saw something that needed protecting and couldn't walk away."

"But you've trained for years. You know so much more than I do."

"Knowledge isn't the same as connection." Finn's voice was quiet now, almost reluctant. "I can tell you how dragons think, what they need, how to read their moods. But I've never formed a Flame-Bind. I've spent three years trying, and the closest I've come is—" He gestured at Spark. "Watching you do it by accident."

Lina stared at him. She had assumed Finn was the expert, the one who knew everything, the one who should be leading. But he was looking at her like she had something he didn't. Something he wanted.

"I don't understand," she said. "If you know so much, why hasn't it worked?"

Finn was quiet for a long moment. When he spoke, his voice was careful, measured—the voice of someone admitting something difficult.

"Because I'm afraid of getting it wrong. The elder who taught me—she told me stories about what happens when bonds break.

Dragons go feral. Humans feel like they've lost something they can never get back." He paused. "I've spent so long trying to do everything right that I've never let myself just—trust."

"But I didn't do anything right," Lina said. "I made mistakes constantly. I didn't know what I was doing."

"Exactly." Something shifted in Finn's expression—not quite a smile, but close. "You weren't trying to follow rules. You were just trying to keep her alive. And she felt that."

They worked with Spark as the sun climbed higher.

Finn showed Lina how to read the dragon's body language—the way her wings shifted when she was curious, the tilt of her head when she was confused, the low rumble in her throat that meant contentment rather than warning. He explained how Emberwings developed their fire control, how flight and flame were connected, how a young dragon needed space to stretch her wings before she could learn to use them properly.

"She needs to fly soon," he said, watching Spark pace the length of the shelter. "Her wings are strong enough. She's just waiting for permission."

"From me?"

"From the bond. She won't do anything that might put you at risk—not until she knows you're ready."

Lina watched Spark move, saw the restless energy in her steps, the way her wings rustled against her sides like they were itching to spread. She thought about all the times she had told the dragon to stay hidden, to keep quiet, to wait.

"I've been holding her back," she said quietly.

"You've been keeping her safe. There's a difference." Finn moved closer to where Spark had stopped, keeping his movements slow and unthreatening. "But she's ready now. The question is whether you are."

Lina thought about the hunters in the region, the patrols, the king's messenger standing in the village square talking about rewards and punishments. Flying meant being visible. Being visible meant being caught.

But keeping Spark grounded meant something else. Finn had said dragons developed fire control through flight. If Spark couldn't fly, she couldn't learn to control her flame. And an Emberwing who couldn't control her fire was a danger to herself and everyone around her.

"How do we do it safely?" Lina asked.

Finn's eyebrows rose slightly. "You're not going to argue?"

"Would it help?"

"No." This time he did smile—brief, surprised. "I thought I'd have to convince you. Explain all the reasons why flight is necessary, cite the old training manuals—"

"She needs it," Lina said simply. "I can feel it. The restlessness, the tension—it's getting worse. If we don't let her fly soon, something's going to break."

Finn studied her for a moment. "That's exactly what the training manuals say. But you didn't need them to know it."

"I know her." Lina shrugged, uncomfortable under his gaze. "That's all."

"That's not all. That's everything." Finn turned back to Spark, who had stopped pacing and was watching them with bright, curious eyes. "The cliffs. Tomorrow, before dawn. There's a cove on the northern side where the rocks block the view from the village. If we time it right, she can fly without being seen."

"And if someone does see?"

"Then we figure it out." Finn's voice was steady, certain. "Together."

They stayed until the light began to fade.

Finn taught her the signals the old trainers used—hand movements that meant come, stay, circle back, land. He showed her how to offer treats to reinforce good behavior, how to stay calm when Spark got overexcited, how to recognize the signs that a dragon was tired and needed rest.

But he also asked questions. What had Lina noticed about Spark's sleeping patterns? How did the dragon react to different foods? What sounds did she make when she was happy, and how were they different from the sounds she made when she was afraid?

"You're testing me," Lina said after the fifth question.

"I'm learning." Finn did not look apologetic. "Every dragon is different. The manuals give general principles, but the details—those come from observation. You've been watching Spark for weeks. You know things I couldn't learn in a year of training."

"I thought you were supposed to be teaching me."

"I am. And you're teaching me." Finn packed up his satchel, movements efficient and practiced. "That's how this works. I have knowledge. You have instinct. Neither one is enough on its own."

Lina thought about that as she watched him prepare to leave. She had come into this believing she needed Finn to tell her what to do, to lead, to be the expert. But he was treating her like an equal—or at least like someone whose observations mattered as much as his training.

It was a strange feeling. Uncomfortable in some ways. But also—

Good. It felt good.

"Same time tomorrow?" Finn asked from the entrance.

"I'll be here."

He nodded and slipped out into the gathering dusk. Lina listened to his footsteps fade, then turned back to Spark.

The dragon was watching her with those knowing amber eyes. The flame in her throat flickered—steady, calm, content.

"Tomorrow," Lina said softly. "Tomorrow you get to fly."

Spark made a sound—low, eager—and her wings rustled against her sides. She understood. Not the words, but the feeling behind them. The promise.

Lina sat back against the wall and let herself breathe. For weeks, she had carried this secret alone, convinced that no one could help her, that asking for help would only make things worse. But now she had Finn. She had knowledge she hadn't possessed yesterday. She had a plan.

It wasn't much. A hidden cove, a pre-dawn flight, two people against a kingdom that wanted dragons dead. But it was more than she'd had before.

She thought about what Finn had said—that the old trainers weren't warriors or chosen ones, just people who couldn't walk away. That knowledge and instinct needed each other. That maybe, together, they had a chance.

She had never meant to be brave. She had only meant to be kind.

But maybe, she was beginning to understand, those weren't as different as she'd always believed.

Spark curled against her side, scales warm, breathing slow. Outside, the wind moved through the pines, carrying the salt-smell of the sea and the first hints of the cold night to come.

Lina closed her eyes and let herself rest.

Tomorrow, everything would change.

But for now, in this moment, she had a dragon who trusted her, a partner who believed in her, and the beginning of something that felt almost like hope.

For now, that was enough.

CHAPTER 7

THE KING OF BONES

The news came with the trading boats.

Lina heard it first from old Marta, who had been down at the docks when the boats arrived from the south. The woman's face was pale, her hands unsteady as she recounted what the traders had told her.

"A public execution," Marta said. "In the square at Ironhold. The king himself presided."

Lina's blood went cold. "A dragon?"

"An Ashback. One of the great ones." Marta's voice dropped to barely a whisper. "They said it took twenty men to bring it down. Chains and nets and those sound-traps that make them go mad. And when they had it—" She stopped, pressing a hand to her mouth.

"What?"

"The king watched it die. Stood there on his platform with his armor on, like he was the one who'd fought it. And when it was done, he gave a speech about safety. About order." Marta's eyes were wet. "They cheered for him, Lina. The whole crowd cheered."

Lina walked away before Marta could say more. Her legs carried her without thought, past the longhouses and the drying racks and the paths she had walked a thousand times. She did not stop until she reached the edge of the Pinewild, where the trees rose dark against the gray sky.

An Ashback. The great protectors, Finn had called them. Dragons who guarded old lands and caves, who rarely bonded but defended those who defended others.

Twenty men to bring it down. Chains and nets. The king watching while it died.

She pressed her back against a pine and tried to breathe.

Finn found her there an hour later.

He came through the trees with his usual careful steps, but his face was tight, his movements sharper than normal. He had heard the news too.

"The traders are talking," he said. "Everyone's talking. An Ashback hasn't been captured in fifteen years."

"Marta said there was a speech."

"There's always a speech." Finn's jaw tightened. "The Sermon of Safe Ash. They recite it before every execution. *'Fear is wisdom.*

Control is mercy. Ash is safety.'" The words came out flat, bitter. "It's propaganda. Dressed up as protection."

Lina thought about the crowd cheering. About people watching a dragon die and calling it victory.

"Why do they believe it?"

"Because it's easier." Finn leaned against the tree beside her, close enough that their shoulders almost touched. "Believing dragons are monsters means you don't have to feel guilty about killing them. Believing the king is keeping you safe means you don't have to take responsibility for what he does in your name."

"But they're not monsters."

"No. They're not." Finn was quiet for a moment. "The traders said something else. The king gave orders after the execution. More hunters. More patrols. He's heard rumors of surviving dragons in the outer regions."

Lina's heart stuttered. "Here?"

"They didn't say specifically. But the eastern reaches were mentioned. That's not far." Finn turned to look at her, his expression serious. "We need to be more careful. Spark's first flight—we should postpone it."

"No."

The word came out before Lina could think. Finn's eyebrows rose.

"You said she needs to fly," Lina continued. "That her fire control depends on it. If we wait—"

"If we wait, she might be safer."

"Or she might lose control and start another fire. One we can't hide." Lina pushed off from the tree, facing him. "The king just killed an Ashback in front of hundreds of people. He's not going to stop. He's never going to stop. And if we keep waiting for a safe moment—" She shook her head. "There isn't going to be one."

Finn studied her. That careful, assessing look she was beginning to know well.

"You've changed," he said.

"What do you mean?"

"A week ago, you would have agreed to wait. You would have wanted to hide, to stay invisible, to hope the danger passed." He paused. "What happened?"

Lina thought about Marta's pale face, about the traders recounting the execution like it was entertainment, about a great dragon brought down by chains and sound-traps while a king watched in his armor.

"I realized hiding doesn't work," she said quietly. "It just means you're alone when they find you."

They went to the shelter together.

Spark was restless when they arrived. She paced the length of the stone floor, wings rustling, small flames flickering in her throat. She had grown again—Lina could see it in the way she held herself, the way her movements had become more confident, more powerful.

"She knows something's wrong," Finn said, watching from just inside the entrance.

"She always knows." Lina crossed to Spark and knelt beside her. The dragon stilled at her touch, amber eyes finding her face. "I'm scared," Lina said softly. "But not of you. Never of you."

Spark pressed her head against Lina's shoulder. The warmth that spread through her chest was familiar now—that sense of connection, of being known without words.

"There was a dragon killed today," Lina continued. "A big one. Far from here, but—" She stopped, unsure how to explain death to a creature who understood emotion but not language.

But Spark seemed to understand anyway. Her flame dimmed. Her body pressed closer. A sound rose from her throat—low, mournful, nothing like the sounds Lina had heard before.

"She feels it," Finn said quietly. He had moved closer, his expression soft in a way Lina hadn't seen before. "Dragons are connected to each other. Not the way they're connected to bonded humans, but—there's something. A sense of loss when one of them dies."

Lina held Spark tighter. She thought about the Ashback dying in chains while a crowd cheered. About Spark growing up in a world where her kind were hunted, hated, destroyed. About what it meant to be one small dragon hiding in a ruined shelter while a king built his power on the bones of her kin.

"We can't let that happen to her," she said.

"We won't."

"You don't know that."

"No," Finn admitted. "I don't. But I know that hiding forever isn't the answer. You were right about that." He paused. "Tomorrow. The cove. We'll be careful, but we won't wait."

Lina nodded, her throat tight.

That night, the village gathered to hear the full account from the traders.

Lina stood at the back of the crowd, half-hidden in shadow, listening to strangers describe what they had seen at Ironhold. The great square filled with people. The platform where the king stood in his black and iron-gray armor. The dragon in chains—massive, ancient, its scales the color of charcoal and molten gold.

"It fought," one trader said. He was a thick-set man with a sailor's weathered face. "Even with the chains, even with the sound-traps screaming, it fought. Killed three hunters before they brought it down."

"Good," someone muttered nearby. Lina didn't see who.

"The king spoke after," the trader continued. "Said the dragon had been terrorizing villages in the southern mountains. Said his hunters had tracked it for months. Said this was proof that his methods work—that dragons can be beaten, can be killed, can be erased from the sky."

"And then?" someone asked.

"Then they burned the body." The trader's voice was flat. "In the square. While everyone watched. And the king said—" He paused, as if remembering the exact words. "'Let this be the last fire any dragon ever lights. Let their flame die with them.'"

A murmur ran through the crowd. Some voices approving, some uncertain. Lina saw her mother standing near the front, arms crossed, face unreadable.

"He's expanding the hunts," another trader added. "Sending more patrols to the outer regions. Says he's heard rumors of surviving dragons. Wants them found and killed before they can breed."

Lina thought of Spark, hidden in the shelter, growing stronger each day. She thought of eggs smashed before they could hatch, of hatchlings killed before they could fly, of a king who wanted to erase an entire species because he feared what they represented.

She slipped away before the gathering ended.

The path to the cliffs was dark, lit only by the stars and the thin sliver of moon rising over the sea. Lina climbed without thinking, her feet finding the familiar holds, her mind still echoing with the trader's words.

At the top, she stood on the flat ledge where she had first seen Finn with a dragon, where everything had begun. The wind pulled at her hair, carrying the salt-smell of the ocean and the cold promise of the coming winter.

She had thought the king was distant. A threat, yes, but a far-off one—something that happened to other people in other places. The hunts had been rumors, the execution stories told by travelers. Even when the messenger came to the village, even when she knew the danger was real, part of her had believed it wouldn't touch her. Wouldn't find her.

But the king had stood in his armor and watched a dragon die. He had ordered more patrols, more hunters, more deaths. He was searching for surviving dragons—searching for eggs before they could hatch, for hatchlings before they could fly.

Searching for Spark.

Lina wrapped her arms around herself and stared out at the dark water. She thought about the Ashback fighting in chains, killing three hunters before the end. She thought about Spark pressing against her side, mourning a dragon she had never met.

She thought about what Finn had said—that dragons were connected, that they sensed when one of their own was lost.

How many had Spark felt die? How many more would she feel before this was over?

The wind gusted, sharp with cold, and Lina let it push against her. She had spent weeks believing that if she was just careful enough, just quiet enough, just invisible enough, she could keep Spark safe. But the king wasn't looking for careful. He was looking for dragons. All of them. Every single one.

And he wasn't going to stop until they were gone.

The threat wasn't distant anymore. It wasn't something that happened to other people. It was here, now, closing in with every patrol the king dispatched, every hunter he trained, every execution he ordered.

Lina stood on the cliffs until her fingers went numb with cold. Then she climbed back down and walked through the dark forest to the shelter.

Spark was waiting.

The dragon lifted her head when Lina entered, her amber eyes catching the faint light. She made a soft sound—welcome, comfort, question—and rose to press against Lina's side.

"I'm here," Lina whispered. She sank down against the wall, and Spark curled beside her, scales warm, breathing slow. "I'm not going anywhere."

The dragon's flame flickered once—steady, trusting—and then settled into darkness.

Lina leaned her head back against the cold stone. Tomorrow, Spark would fly for the first time. Tomorrow, everything would change again. But tonight, in this moment, they were together.

And somewhere far to the south, a king sat in his fortress of black stone and iron, planning the extinction of everything Lina had come to love.

CHAPTER 8

WHAT HUNTERS LEAVE BEHIND

S park flew at dawn.

Lina stood in the hidden cove, her back pressed against the cliff face, and watched her dragon rise into the pale morning sky. Spark's wings caught the air with an instinct that needed no teaching—up, up, spiraling against the gray clouds until she was a dark shape moving through the light.

"She's a natural," Finn said quietly. He stood beside Lina, his eyes tracking Spark's flight. "Some dragons take weeks to find their balance. She's had it from the start."

Lina could not speak. Her throat was tight with something that felt like joy and terror twisted together. Spark was flying. Spark was free, for the first time in her life, moving through the sky the way she was meant to.

And anyone who looked up might see her.

"Call her back," Finn said. "Three circles, then down. That's enough for today."

Lina raised her hand and made the signal Finn had taught her—a slow, sweeping motion that meant return. For a moment, nothing happened. Spark continued to climb, wings beating steadily, and Lina felt a spike of fear that the dragon would keep going, would fly too high, too far, too visible—

Then Spark turned. She circled once, twice, three times, and began her descent.

She landed clumsily, her claws scraping against the rocks, her wings folding at an awkward angle. But she was down. She was safe. And the look in her amber eyes when she pressed her head against Lina's chest was pure, unfiltered happiness.

"Good girl," Lina whispered, her hands finding the warm ridges above Spark's eyes. "You did it. You flew."

Spark made a sound—something between a purr and a croon—and a small, steady flame flickered in her throat. Trust. Contentment. Joy.

"Tomorrow we'll try longer," Finn said. "Build her endurance. Work on her landings." He paused, and something shifted in his expression. "She's going to be strong, Lina. When she's fully grown—"

He didn't finish. He didn't need to.

When Spark was fully grown, she would be impossible to hide.

They smelled the smoke before they saw it.

Lina was halfway back to the village, Spark safely hidden in the shelter, when the wind shifted and brought the scent—not woodsmoke, not cooking fire, but something sharper. Heavier. Wrong.

"That's not from the village," Finn said. He had stopped on the path, his head tilted, his body suddenly tense. "It's coming from the east."

The east. The forest. The direction of the old mountain paths that led deeper into the wild lands.

They ran.

The smoke thickened as they climbed the ridge above the Pinewild. Lina's lungs burned, her legs ached, but she did not slow. Something was wrong—something was very, very wrong—and she needed to see what it was.

They crested the ridge and stopped.

Below them, in a clearing that Lina had passed a dozen times on her way to the shelter, the hunters had made camp. Three tents. A fire pit. Horses tied to a makeshift post.

And in the center of the clearing, still smoking, lay the remains of a dragon.

Lina's stomach heaved. The dragon was small—not a hatchling, but young, maybe a year or two old. Its scales had been green once, the dark green of a Windrunner, but now they were blackened and cracked, ruined by fire that had not come from within. Its wings were shredded. Its eyes were open, clouded, empty.

"They burned it," she whispered. "They killed it and then they burned it."

Finn's hand closed on her arm. "Lina—"

"Why would they burn it?" Her voice was rising, and she couldn't stop it. "It was already dead. Why would they—"

"To send a message." Finn's voice was flat, controlled, but Lina could hear the strain beneath it. "They do this when they want people to know they're in the area. Burn the body, leave it where it can be found. It's a warning."

"A warning to whom?"

"To anyone hiding dragons. Anyone protecting them." Finn pulled her back from the ridge, into the cover of the trees. "We need to go. If they see us—"

"No."

The word came out hard, sharp. Lina pulled her arm free and turned back toward the clearing. The hunters were visible now—four men in the king's colors, sitting around their fire, laughing at something one of them had said.

Laughing. While a dragon's body smoked ten feet away from them.

"They're laughing," Lina said. Her hands had curled into fists. "They killed it and burned it and now they're laughing."

"Lina." Finn was beside her again, his voice low and urgent. "I know. I know how this feels. But we can't—"

"Can't what? Can't be angry? Can't hate them?" She spun to face him. "That was someone's dragon, Finn. Maybe it had a bond. Maybe someone loved it. And they killed it and burned it and they're sitting there laughing like it was nothing."

"I know."

"Then why are you so calm?"

Finn was quiet for a moment. When he spoke, his voice was steady, but his eyes were not.

"Because I've seen this before," he said. "More times than I can count. And I've learned that anger doesn't help. It just makes you careless."

"So we do nothing?"

"We stay alive." Finn's hand found her shoulder, firm but not unkind. "We go back to the shelter. We make sure Spark is safe. And we don't give those men any reason to look in our direction."

Lina looked back at the clearing. At the hunters laughing by their fire. At the ruined body of a dragon who had done nothing wrong except exist in a world that wanted it dead.

She wanted to scream. She wanted to run down there and make them pay for what they had done. She wanted to call Spark and watch them burn the way they had burned that Windrunner.

But Finn was right. Anger wouldn't help. It would only get them caught.

"Fine," she said, the word bitter on her tongue. "We go."

The village was different when they returned.

Lina noticed it immediately—the tension in the air, the way people moved with their heads down and their voices low. Something had happened while they were gone.

She found her mother outside their longhouse, scrubbing clothes with more force than necessary.

"The hunters came," her mother said without looking up. "Searched three houses. Said they were looking for signs of dragon sympathizers."

Lina's blood went cold. "Which houses?"

"The Erikssons. Old Marta. The widow by the docks." Her mother's hands stilled on the cloth. "They didn't find anything. But they made it clear they'd be back."

Old Marta. The woman who had told Lina about the execution at Ironhold. The woman whose face had been pale with horror at what the king had done.

"Why those houses?"

"Someone talked." Her mother's voice was flat. "Someone told them Marta spoke against the hunts. That the Erikssons had refused to join the last patrol. That the widow's husband used to work with dragons, before the purge."

Someone talked. Someone in the village had reported their neighbors to the king's hunters.

"Who?"

"Does it matter?" Her mother finally looked up, and Lina saw the fear in her eyes—fear she was trying hard to hide. "The hunters are here now. They're watching. And anyone who gives them a reason to look closer—" She stopped, shook her head. "Just stay quiet, Lina. Stay invisible. That's how we survive this."

Stay quiet. Stay invisible.

The words echoed in Lina's head as she walked away from her mother. They were the same words she had lived by her whole life. The same words she had told herself when she first found Spark's egg. Keep your head down. Don't draw attention. Let the danger pass.

But staying quiet hadn't helped Marta. Hadn't helped the Erikssons or the widow. They had kept their heads down, and someone had reported them anyway.

Silence wasn't safety. It was just a different kind of trap.

She found Finn at the shelter.

He was sitting with Spark, speaking to her in that low, calm voice he used when he wanted a dragon to feel safe. Spark's head was resting on his knee—not the easy intimacy she shared with Lina, but something close to acceptance.

"She knows," Finn said when Lina entered. "About the Windrunner. She's been restless since we got back."

"How?"

"I told you—dragons sense each other. When one dies, especially one nearby—" He shook his head. "She felt it."

Lina crossed to them and sank down beside Spark. The dragon lifted her head and pressed it against Lina's shoulder, making that low, mournful sound she had made when she learned about the Ashback at Ironhold.

Two dragons dead in as many days. Both killed by hunters. Both burned for show.

"The hunters searched the village," Lina said. "Three houses. Someone reported them for speaking against the hunts."

Finn's expression darkened. "It's how the system works. Turn neighbors against each other. Make everyone afraid to speak, afraid to trust. Eventually, people stop protecting each other and start protecting themselves."

"My mother told me to stay quiet. Stay invisible." Lina's voice was bitter. "But those people were quiet. They were invisible. And it didn't help."

"No," Finn agreed. "It doesn't."

"Then what's the point?" Lina looked at him, something breaking open in her chest. "What's the point of staying silent if silence doesn't protect anyone? If the hunters are going to search and the dragons are going to die and the king is going to keep sending more patrols until there's nothing left?"

Finn was quiet for a long moment. Spark shifted between them, her scales warm against Lina's side.

"The point," he said finally, "is that we're not silent. Not anymore." He met her eyes. "You're not hiding because you think it will save you. You're hiding because Spark isn't ready yet. Because we need more time to figure out what comes next."

"And what does come next?"

"I don't know." The admission seemed to cost him something. "I've spent three years keeping my head down, doing what the elder taught me, hoping that if I was just careful enough, I could save a few dragons without anyone noticing." He paused. "But you're right. Careful isn't enough anymore. The king is escalating. He's not going to stop until every dragon is dead and everyone who helped them is punished."

"So we fight."

"Not yet." Finn held up a hand before she could protest. "I'm not saying never. I'm saying not yet. Spark needs to be stronger. We need to be smarter. And we need to understand what we're fighting against."

"A king who burns dragons for show."

"More than that." Finn's voice was serious now, weighted with something Lina didn't fully understand. "A system. A belief. The idea that fear is the only thing that keeps people safe. That's what we're fighting. And you can't defeat an idea with anger alone."

Lina thought about the hunters laughing in the clearing. About Marta's house being searched because she spoke against cruelty. About a kingdom built on the bones of dragons and the silence of everyone too afraid to say no.

"Then what do we defeat it with?"

Finn looked at Spark, at the small dragon curled between them with her steady flame and her trusting eyes.

"Proof," he said. "Proof that dragons aren't monsters. That they can be trusted. That fire doesn't have to mean destruction." He turned back to Lina. "That's what Spark is. That's why she matters. Not because she's one dragon we can save, but because she's proof that everything the king believes is wrong."

Proof.

Lina looked at Spark—at the dragon who had chosen her, who trusted her, who had flown for the first time that morning and landed with joy in her eyes.

She thought about what it would mean to show that to others. To let people see what she had seen. To offer them something besides fear.

It was dangerous. It was probably impossible. It went against everything she had ever been taught about survival.

But it was also, she realized, the only thing that might actually work.

"Okay," she said quietly. "We wait. We train. We get stronger." She met Finn's eyes. "But not forever. And not in silence."

Finn nodded slowly. "Not forever. And not in silence."

Spark raised her head and made a sound—not mournful this time, but something else. Something that might have been agreement.

Outside, the sun was setting, painting the sky in shades of fire. Somewhere in the forest, hunters were making camp beside the body of a dragon they had killed. And in the village below, people were learning to fear their neighbors, to stay quiet, to hope the danger would pass them by.

But in this shelter, hidden in the pines, something different was growing.

Not just a dragon learning to fly.

A rebellion learning to breathe.

CHAPTER 9

THE FLAME-BOND

Three days had passed of careful flights in the hidden cove, of watching Spark grow stronger and more confident with each passing hour. Three days of training with Finn, learning the signals and the rhythms and the quiet language that existed between dragon and human.

Three days of pretending, in the village, that nothing had changed.

The hunters had moved on—their camp in the clearing was empty now, the Windrunner's burned remains covered by a thin layer of frost. But the fear they had left behind still lingered in the village like smoke that would not clear. People spoke in whispers. Neighbors watched each other with suspicious eyes. And Lina's mother had taken to checking the door three times each night before she would sleep.

"They'll be back," Finn said on the fourth morning. They were sitting in the shelter, watching Spark pace the length of the stone floor. "The patrols are getting more frequent. Someone in the capital is pushing for results."

"The king."

"Probably." Finn's expression was troubled. "The traders say he's obsessed with finding the last dragons. That he won't rest until every egg is smashed and every hatchling is dead."

Lina watched Spark move. The dragon had changed in the past few days—grown larger, more graceful, her wings folding and unfolding with an ease that spoke of muscles finally learning their purpose. Her scales had darkened further, charcoal deepening to something almost black, with those copper undertones flashing like hidden fire when the light caught them right.

She was beautiful. And every day she became harder to hide.

"We should fly today," Lina said. "While the weather holds."

Finn nodded, but something in his expression made her pause.

"What?"

"I've been thinking," he said slowly. "About what happens next. Spark is almost ready—her flight is strong, her fire is controlled, her instincts are sharp. But she's still young. If the hunters find her now, she won't be able to defend herself."

"So we keep hiding her."

"For how long?" Finn met her eyes. "A month? A year? She's going to keep growing, Lina. By spring, she'll be the size of a horse. By next winter, she'll be bigger than this shelter. We can't hide her forever."

Lina knew he was right. She had known it since the first time she watched Spark fly—that moment of joy undercut by the cold knowledge that flight meant visibility, and visibility meant death.

"Then what do we do?"

"I don't know yet." The admission seemed to cost him something. "But I think we need to start planning. Not just for tomorrow, or next week. For the future."

Spark stopped pacing. Her head turned toward them, amber eyes moving from Finn's face to Lina's, and she made a sound—low, questioning, uncertain.

"She knows we're worried," Lina said.

"She always knows."

The flight that morning was different.

Lina felt it from the moment Spark launched into the air. There was a tension in the dragon's movements, a restlessness that went beyond the usual joy of flight. She circled higher than before, pushing against the limits Finn had set, testing the boundaries of the cove's sheltered space.

"She wants to go further," Finn said, his eyes tracking Spark's spiraling ascent. "She's ready."

"But—"

"I know. It's not safe." He paused. "Call her down. We'll try again tomorrow."

Lina raised her hand to make the signal, but before she could complete it, Spark did something unexpected.

She dove.

Not toward the landing spot they had practiced, but straight toward Lina. Wings folded tight against her body, scales catching the morning light, she plummeted like a falling star—and Lina's heart stopped, because Spark was coming too fast, too steep; there was no way she could pull up in time—

Spark's wings snapped open three feet from the ground. The force of her stop sent a gust of wind washing over Lina's face, warm with dragon-heat, and then Spark was there, hovering, her amber eyes locked on Lina's with an intensity that took her breath away.

"What—" Lina started.

Spark landed. Gently, precisely, her claws finding purchase on the rocky ground with none of the clumsiness of her early attempts. She folded her wings and stepped forward, pressing her head against Lina's chest.

And then something happened that Lina could not explain.

Warmth spread through her. Not physical warmth, though Spark's scales were hot against her skin. Something deeper. Something that started in her chest and radiated outward until it filled every part of her—a feeling of connection, of recognition, of being known completely and accepted entirely.

She felt Spark's heart beating. Not hearing it—feeling it, as if it were her own pulse, doubled.

She felt Spark's emotions washing through her. Joy. Trust. Determination. A fierce, protective love that burned like fire but did not consume.

And beneath all of it, a single, clear intention: *Mine. You are mine, and I am yours, and nothing will ever change that.*

Lina's eyes filled with tears. She wrapped her arms around Spark's neck and held on, feeling the dragon's warmth seep into her bones, feeling the bond that had been growing between them since the moment she first touched that smooth, warm egg finally settle into place.

"Lina." Finn's voice was strange—hushed, almost reverent. "Do you feel that?"

She couldn't speak. She could only nod, her face pressed against Spark's scales, tears running down her cheeks.

"That's the Flame-Bind," Finn said. "The real one. I've read about it, heard stories, but I've never—" He stopped, and when Lina looked up, she saw that his eyes were bright too. "She chose you. Fully. Completely. There's no going back now."

They sat in the cove for a long time after.

Spark curled around Lina like a protective wall, her head resting in Lina's lap, her breathing slow and content. The bond pulsed between them—not overwhelming anymore, but present, a constant awareness of each other that felt as natural as breathing.

"What does it mean?" Lina asked. Her voice was hoarse. "The Flame-Bind. What does it actually do?"

Finn sat across from her, his back against the cliff face. He had been watching them with an expression Lina couldn't quite read—wonder, maybe, or something close to envy.

"It's a partnership," he said. "Not control—the bond doesn't let you command her. But you'll be able to sense each other. Her emotions, her needs, her warnings. And she'll sense yours."

"I felt her heart beating."

"That's part of it. The bond connects you physically as well as emotionally. If she's hurt, you'll feel an echo of it. If you're in danger, she'll know." Finn paused. "The old trainers said that a Flame-Bind pair could communicate without words. Not speech, exactly, but—understanding. Intent. They moved together like one being in two bodies."

Lina stroked the ridge above Spark's eyes. The dragon made a soft sound and pressed closer.

"You said she chose me. What if I hadn't—" She stopped, unsure how to finish the question.

"Hadn't chosen her back?" Finn shook his head. "The bond is voluntary on both sides. If you had rejected her—if you had been afraid, or unwilling—it wouldn't have formed. The fact that it did means you chose her too. Maybe before you even realized you were choosing."

Lina thought about the night she found the egg. The moment she decided to save it instead of leaving it to the cold. She had told herself it was just kindness, just instinct, just doing what anyone would do.

But maybe it had been more than that. Maybe, in that moment, she had made a choice she didn't fully understand. A choice that would bind her to this dragon—this fierce, loyal, trusting creature—for the rest of her life.

"Is it permanent?" she asked.

"Yes." Finn's voice was serious. "Once a Flame-Bind forms, it can't be undone. Not without—" He hesitated. "Not without great cost. To both of you."

"What happens if it breaks?"

"The dragon goes feral. Loses the ability to trust, to connect. Becomes what the king says all dragons are—wild, dangerous, unpredictable." Finn met her eyes. "And the human feels it. A loss that never heals. Like grief that has no name."

Lina looked down at Spark. The dragon's eyes were closed, her breathing even, her flame a steady glow in her throat. She looked peaceful. Safe. Loved.

"Then we don't let it break," Lina said.

"It's not that simple. If the hunters find you—if they capture her, or kill her—"

"Then we don't let them find us." Lina's voice was steady, certain. She felt the bond pulsing in her chest, felt Spark's presence like a second heartbeat, and something settled into place inside her. "I chose her, Finn. She chose me. Whatever comes next, we face it together."

That evening, Lina stayed at the shelter longer than usual.

Finn had returned to the village, promising to bring food and check for news of more patrols. But Lina couldn't bring herself to leave. The bond was still new, still overwhelming in its intensity, and being away from Spark felt wrong in a way she couldn't explain.

So she sat with her dragon as the light faded, feeling the warmth of Spark's scales against her side, watching the flame flicker in the dragon's throat—steady, calm, content.

"I didn't know," she said softly. "When I found you. I didn't know what it would mean. I just saw something that needed help, and I couldn't walk away."

Spark made a sound—that low, rumbling croon that meant comfort, understanding, love.

"I was so afraid. I thought I was doing everything wrong. I thought someone else should be taking care of you—someone braver, someone who knew what they were doing." Lina laughed quietly. "I still think that, sometimes. That I'm not good enough. Not strong enough."

Spark lifted her head. Her amber eyes found Lina's face, and through the bond, Lina felt a pulse of emotion—fierce, protective, certain.

You, the feeling said. *Only you. Always you.*

Lina's throat tightened. She had spent her whole life believing she was ordinary. Unremarkable. The kind of person who faded into the background while others did the important things.

But Spark didn't see her that way. Through the bond, Lina could feel how the dragon saw her—not as someone small or weak or forgettable, but as someone who had chosen protection over fear, kindness over safety, love over self-preservation.

Someone worth binding to. Someone worth trusting with everything.

"I won't let them hurt you," Lina whispered. "Whatever happens. Whatever it costs. I will keep you safe."

Spark pressed her head against Lina's chest. The flame in her throat brightened—not with fear or warning, but with something else. Something that felt like a promise being made.

Through the bond, Lina felt the response: *And I will keep you safe. We are one now. We protect each other.*

Outside, the wind moved through the pines, carrying the first bite of true winter. Somewhere in the distance, a wolf howled, and another answered. The world was full of dangers—hunters and kings and people who would destroy what they feared.

But in this shelter, wrapped in warmth and connection and the fierce certainty of a bond that could not be broken, Lina felt something she had not felt in a long time.

Hope.

Not the fragile hope she had clung to before—the hope that danger would pass, that hiding would be enough, that she could survive by staying small and invisible. This was something stronger. Something that burned.

She had been chosen. Not because she was brave or strong or special, but because she had chosen first. Because she had looked at something the world wanted to destroy and decided to protect it instead.

And now she was not alone.

Lina closed her eyes and let the bond settle into her bones. She felt Spark's heartbeat alongside her own, felt the warmth of dragon-fire burning steadily in the darkness, felt the weight of what she had become.

Not just a girl hiding a dragon.

A girl bound to one.

Whatever came next, they would face it together.

And that, she was beginning to understand, made all the difference.

CHAPTER 10

NO SAFE GROUND

The soldiers came at dawn.

Lina woke to the sound of horses—not the steady plod of traders' mounts, but the sharp, disciplined rhythm of warhorses moving in formation. She was on her feet before she was fully awake, her heart hammering, the bond with Spark flaring bright with sudden alarm.

Through the small window of the longhouse, she saw them. A column of riders in the king's colors—black and iron-gray—streaming into the village from the southern road. Twenty soldiers, maybe more. Their armor caught the pale morning light, and the banner at their head bore the king's crest: a sword thrust through a dragon's skull.

"Lina." Her mother's voice came from behind her, tight with fear. "Get away from the window."

"They're searching," Lina said. Her voice sounded distant, strange. "They're going to search everything."

"We have nothing to hide." Her mother crossed to her, gripping her arm. "Do you understand? We have nothing to hide. You've been gathering kindling in the forest, helping with the nets, doing your chores. That's all."

Lina looked at her mother—at the fear barely concealed behind her stern expression—and felt the bond pulse in her chest. Spark was awake now, fully alert, her anxiety threading through Lina's blood like fire.

"That's all," Lina repeated. The lie tasted like ash.

The soldiers worked methodically.

Lina watched from the doorway of the longhouse as they moved through the village—two or three to each building, searching storage cellars and lofts, overturning crates, questioning anyone who crossed their path. Their captain was a broad-shouldered man with a scar running from his temple to his jaw, and he directed his men with short, sharp commands that left no room for argument.

"Looking for dragon sympathizers," old Marta muttered. She appeared beside Lina without warning, her weathered face drawn tight. "That's what they told Erik when they searched his house. Said they had reports of suspicious activity in the region."

"Reports from whom?"

"Does it matter?" Marta's voice was bitter. "Could be anyone. Could be no one. The king doesn't need proof anymore—just suspicion."

A soldier approached the longhouse, and Lina's mother stepped forward, positioning herself between him and her daughter.

"This dwelling is registered to Kara," the soldier said, consulting a list. "Widow. One daughter."

"That's right." Her mother's voice was steady, but Lina could see her hands trembling at her sides.

"We'll need to search the premises. Step aside."

It wasn't a request. Lina's mother moved, and the soldier pushed past her into the longhouse. A second soldier followed. They moved through the small space with brutal efficiency—lifting bedding, checking corners, pulling open the chest where Lina's mother kept their few valuables.

"What are you looking for?" Lina asked. She had meant to stay quiet, to be invisible, but the words came out before she could stop them.

The soldier nearest her—young, barely older than Finn—gave her a flat look. "Dragon sign. Eggs. Scales. Anything that doesn't belong."

"There's nothing like that here."

"Then you have nothing to worry about." He turned back to his search, and Lina felt her mother's hand close around her wrist. *Stay quiet. Stay small. Let them finish.*

Through the bond, Spark's anxiety sharpened into something closer to fear. Lina closed her eyes and tried to send reassurance—calm, safety, stay hidden—but she didn't know if it worked. The bond was still new, still unpredictable. She could feel Spark's emotions, but she didn't know if Spark could feel hers in return.

The soldiers finished their search and left without a word. They moved to the next longhouse, and the next, working their way through the village with the same cold precision.

Lina's mother sagged against the door frame. "They didn't find anything. We're safe."

But Lina was watching the captain. He stood in the center of the village, surveying his men's work, and his gaze swept across the buildings, the paths, the forest rising dark behind them.

The forest. Where the shelter was. Where Spark was hiding.

"They're not done," Lina said quietly. "They're going to search the forest too."

She found Finn at the edge of the village.

He was standing behind a storage shed, watching the soldiers with careful, measuring eyes. When he saw Lina approaching, his expression tightened.

"I know," he said before she could speak. "I've been watching since they arrived."

"They're going to search the forest."

"Yes." Finn's jaw was tight. "The captain sent scouts into the Pinewild an hour ago. Small groups, spreading out to cover more ground."

Lina's blood went cold. "The shelter—"

"It's not on any maps. Most people don't even know it exists. But if they're thorough—" He didn't finish. He didn't need to.

"We have to move her."

"Where? The soldiers are everywhere. If we try to take her out now, someone will see."

Through the bond, Lina felt Spark's fear spike. The dragon knew something was wrong—could feel Lina's panic bleeding through their connection. If she got scared enough, if she lost control of her flame—

"I have to go to her," Lina said. "If she panics—"

"If you go into the forest now, they'll follow you." Finn caught her arm, holding her in place. "Think, Lina. You're a village girl who suddenly needs to visit the Pinewild while soldiers are searching for dragons? They'll watch every step you take."

"Then what do we do?"

Finn was quiet for a long moment. His eyes moved across the village—the soldiers, the frightened villagers, the forest rising dark and dangerous beyond.

"We wait," he said finally. "Until dark. Then we move her."

"Move her where?"

"The mountains." His voice was low, urgent. "The Highspine range. There are caves there—old dragon nesting grounds. The king's men don't go that far. It's too remote, too dangerous."

"That's two days' journey on foot."

"Three, if we're careful." Finn met her eyes. "But Spark can fly now. She could make it in hours."

"Alone?"

"No." Something shifted in Finn's expression—resolution, maybe, or acceptance. "Not alone. We go with her. Tonight. All three of us."

Lina stared at him. "You mean leave. Leave the village. Leave everything."

"I mean survive." Finn's voice was hard. "The soldiers aren't going to stop, Lina. They're not going to search once and then leave us alone. They'll keep coming back, keep watching, keep looking for any sign that we're hiding something. And eventually—" He stopped, took a breath. "Eventually, they'll find her. Or someone will talk. Or we'll make a mistake. And when that happens, it won't just be Spark they kill. It will be us too."

The words hung in the air between them. Lina thought about her mother, about the longhouse, about the life she had always known. She thought about morning fog on the water and the smell of fish drying on the racks and the sound of her neighbors' voices calling to each other across the village square.

All of it, gone. If she left tonight, she might never see any of it again.

But through the bond, she felt Spark—afraid, alone, waiting in the darkness of the shelter for danger she could sense but not see.

And she knew, with a certainty that went deeper than thought, that she could not abandon her dragon. Not for home. Not for safety. Not for anything.

"Tonight," she said. "We leave tonight."

The day passed in agonizing slowness.

Lina went through the motions of ordinary life—helping her mother mend nets, carrying water from the well, pretending that nothing had changed. All the while, she felt Spark through the bond, a constant presence of fear and confusion and desperate, aching loneliness.

I'm coming, she thought, over and over, hoping Spark could feel it. *Hold on. I'm coming.*

The soldiers continued their search. She saw groups returning from the forest throughout the afternoon—muddy, frustrated, empty-handed. The shelter had not been found. Not yet.

But they would keep looking. The captain had made that clear. He had gathered the village at midday, standing on the steps of the meeting hall with his scarred face set in grim lines, and delivered a warning.

"We have reason to believe dragons are being hidden in this region," he said. "Anyone found aiding these creatures—sheltering them, feeding them, protecting them in any way—will be executed as a traitor to the crown. The king's mercy does not extend to those who side with monsters."

Lina had stood in the crowd, her mother's hand tight on her arm, and felt the words settle into her like stones.

Executed as a traitor.

She had known the risk, of course. Finn had told her the punishment on the day they first spoke. But hearing it now—from a soldier in the king's colors, in the village where she had grown up, surrounded by neighbors who might turn her in if they knew—made it real in a way it hadn't been before.

This was her life now. Not the girl who gathered kindling and mended nets and dreamed of nothing more than an ordinary existence. She was a dragon keeper. A traitor to the crown. A fugitive.

And after tonight, there would be no going back.

She told her mother at sunset.

Not everything—not about Spark, not about the bond, not about the weeks of secret visits to the shelter in the forest. Just that she had to leave. That she had to go tonight, and she didn't know when she would be back.

Her mother listened in silence. When Lina finished, she was quiet for a long moment, her face turned toward the window, the dying light painting her features in shades of gold and shadow.

"You've been different lately," she said finally. "Disappearing into the forest. Coming home with that look in your eyes—like you're carrying something too heavy for you." She turned to face Lina. "I told myself it was nothing. Told myself you were just growing up, finding your own way. But it's not nothing, is it?"

Lina's throat tightened. "No."

"And I shouldn't ask what it is."

"It's safer if you don't know."

Her mother nodded slowly. The acceptance in her eyes was worse, somehow, than anger would have been. "You're doing something good, aren't you? Something that matters."

"I'm trying to."

"Then go." Her mother crossed to her and took her face in her hands—rough, work-worn hands that had held Lina since the day she was born. "Go, and be careful, and come back to me when you can." Her voice cracked on the last words. "Promise me you'll come back."

"I promise." The words felt like a lie and a prayer all at once.

Her mother pulled her close and held her—just for a moment, a single breath of warmth and safety—and then let her go.

"Go," she said again. "Before I change my mind."

The forest was dark.

Lina moved through the trees by feel, following paths she had memorized over weeks of secret visits. The soldiers had retreated to their camp for the night, but she knew they had left watchers—she could sense them, somehow, feel the wrongness of their presence in woods that should have been empty.

She found Finn waiting at the edge of a clearing. He had a pack over his shoulder and a grim set to his jaw.

"There are two sentries between here and the shelter," he whispered. "I watched their patterns. We have maybe ten minutes before they circle back."

They moved together, silent as shadows, slipping between the pines on paths that were more instinct than memory. The bond pulsed in Lina's chest—stronger now, urgent, pulling her toward Spark like a thread she could follow in the dark.

The shelter appeared before them, half-collapsed walls rising from the forest floor. Lina ducked through the entrance and found Spark pressed against the far wall, her amber eyes wide, her scales rippling with barely contained heat.

"I'm here," Lina breathed, crossing to her. "I'm here. It's all right."

Spark surged forward, pressing her head against Lina's chest. Through the bond, Lina felt the dragon's relief—overwhelming, consuming, like a wave breaking against the shore. *Safe. You came. You're here.*

"We have to go," Finn said from the entrance. "Now. Before the sentries return."

Lina looked at Spark. The dragon was bigger now—too big to hide in a corner, too big to pretend she was anything other than what she was. Her wings stretched wide when she moved, brushing the walls of the shelter that had once seemed so spacious.

"Can you fly?" Lina asked her. "Can you carry us both?"

Spark's response came through the bond—not words, but feeling. Determination. Certainty. *Yes. I can. I will.*

"Then let's go."

They slipped out of the shelter and into the night. The forest pressed close around them, dark and cold, full of dangers seen and unseen. Somewhere behind them, soldiers waited with weapons and chains. Somewhere ahead, mountains rose into clouds that promised snow.

And between them, moving through the darkness toward an uncertain future, a girl and her dragon took their first steps into a world that wanted them dead.

Hiding was over.

The running had begun.

CHAPTER 11

THE BURNING

They made it less than a mile before the hunters found them.

Lina heard the dogs first—that sharp, eager baying that meant prey had been scented. Then torchlight flickered between the trees, orange and angry against the darkness, and voices called to each other in the clipped tones of soldiers on a hunt.

"They've found our trail," Finn said. His face was pale in the moonlight, his eyes scanning the forest ahead. "The dogs must have picked up Spark's scent at the shelter."

Through the bond, Lina felt Spark's fear spike—wild, primal, the terror of a creature that knew it was being hunted. The dragon pressed close to her side, scales hot with barely contained fire, wings trembling against her body.

"She needs to fly," Lina said. "Now. Before they get closer."

"If she takes off, they'll see her. The torches will light her up like a beacon."

"If she stays on the ground, they'll catch her." Lina's voice was sharper than she meant it to be. The dogs were closer now—she could hear them crashing through the underbrush, their handlers shouting encouragement. "We don't have a choice, Finn."

A horn sounded somewhere behind them. Three short blasts—a signal. More shouts answered, spreading through the forest like fire through dry kindling.

"They're surrounding us," Finn said. "Trying to box us in."

Lina looked at Spark. The dragon's eyes were wide, her flame flickering erratically in her throat—fear and anger and desperation all tangled together. Through the bond, Lina felt her dragon's overwhelming urge to run, to fight, to do something.

"There's a clearing ahead," Finn said. "Half a minute's run. If we can reach it before they close the circle—"

"Go," Lina said. "We'll be right behind you."

Finn hesitated for a moment, then nodded and ran. Lina turned to Spark, placed her hands on either side of the dragon's face, and looked into those frightened amber eyes.

"Listen to me," she said. Her voice was steady, calmer than she felt. "We're going to get out of this. But I need you to trust me. Can you do that?"

Through the bond, Spark's fear shifted—not disappearing, but changing shape. Becoming something she could hold alongside the terror instead of being consumed by it.

Trust, the feeling said. *Always.*

"Then run."

They burst into the clearing just as the first soldiers emerged from the trees.

Lina saw them in flashes—torchlight on armor, the glint of drawn swords, the dark shapes of dogs straining at their leads. Six men, maybe seven, spreading out to block the far side of the clearing. More coming from behind.

"There!" someone shouted. "The dragon—I see it!"

Spark's wings flared open, and for one terrible moment, she was fully visible—scales gleaming copper and black in the torchlight, eyes reflecting the flames like mirrors. A hunter raised a crossbow. Another pulled something from his belt—a net, Lina realized, weighted with iron at the edges.

"Spark, fly!" Lina screamed.

The dragon launched into the air just as the crossbow bolt sang past. The net followed, spreading wide, its iron weights whistling through the darkness—but Spark was already climbing, wings beating furiously, and the net fell short, tangling uselessly in the branches below.

"Reload!" the hunter shouted. "Don't let it get away!"

But Lina wasn't watching the hunters anymore. She was watching Spark—watching her dragon spiral upward into the dark sky, wings catching the moonlight, finally free of the trees that had hidden her for so long.

And then she felt it through the bond. Not fear anymore. Rage.

Spark turned in the air. Her wings folded. She dove.

"No!" Lina shouted, but it was too late.

Fire erupted from Spark's throat—not the small, controlled flame Lina had seen before, but something vast and terrible, a torrent of orange and gold that lit the clearing like daylight. It struck the ground between Lina and the hunters, and the world exploded into heat and light and chaos.

Men screamed. Dogs howled. The trees at the clearing's edge caught fire, their dry winter branches igniting like kindling. Within seconds, the flames had spread—racing up the trunks, leaping from crown to crown, turning the forest into an inferno.

"Spark!" Lina's voice was lost in the roar of the flames. Through the bond, she felt her dragon's emotions—protective fury, desperate love, the overwhelming need to destroy anything that threatened what was hers.

The hunters were retreating, driven back by the wall of fire. But the flames weren't stopping. They were spreading, consuming everything in their path, and Lina realized with horror that she and Finn were trapped between the soldiers and the blaze.

"Lina!" Finn grabbed her arm, pulling her back from the advancing fire. "We have to move!"

But Lina wasn't listening. She was staring up at Spark, who circled above the inferno she had created, and she was reaching through the bond with everything she had.

Stop, she thought. *Please. You're going to kill us all.*

The fire raged.

Heat pressed against Lina's skin, stealing the breath from her lungs. Smoke burned her eyes, her throat, making it impossible to see more than a few feet in any direction. Somewhere in the chaos, she could hear the hunters shouting—retreating, maybe, or regrouping for another attack.

None of it mattered. All that mattered was Spark.

Through the bond, Lina could feel her dragon's emotions shifting—the rage still burning, but something else beneath it now. Confusion. Fear. The dawning realization that the fire she had started was not stopping, was not obeying, was destroying everything without discrimination.

She's losing control, Lina realized. *She doesn't know how to stop it.*

Lina closed her eyes. The heat was unbearable, the smoke choking, but she forced herself to breathe, to find that place of calm at the center of her terror. She thought of the shelter in the forest—the quiet hours spent with Spark, learning to understand each other. She thought of the bond forming, that moment of absolute connection when everything else fell away.

She thought of what Finn had told her, what felt like a lifetime ago: Dragons don't need us to be fearless. They need us to be true.

I'm afraid, she sent through the bond. *I'm afraid we're going to die here. But I'm not going to run. I'm not going to leave you.*

She opened her eyes and looked up at the sky, at the dark shape circling through the smoke and flames.

"Come down," she said. Her voice was hoarse, barely audible over the roar of the fire. "Come down to me. We'll face this together."

For a long, terrible moment, nothing happened. The fire continued to spread. The smoke continued to rise. Lina felt her consciousness wavering, her body weakening from the heat and the lack of air.

Then Spark dove.

She came down through the flames like a falling star, wings tucked tight, scales gleaming with reflected fire. She landed in front of Lina with a grace that seemed impossible in the chaos, and she pressed her head against Lina's chest, making that low, mournful sound that meant distress, meant apology, meant *I'm sorry, I'm sorry, I didn't mean to.*

"I know," Lina whispered. She wrapped her arms around Spark's neck, feeling the heat of her scales, the rapid pulse of her heart. "I know. It's all right. We're going to be all right."

Through the bond, she felt something shift. Spark's panic easing. Her rage cooling. And with it, impossibly, the fire around them began to change.

The flames didn't stop—they were too far gone for that. But they... softened, somehow. Drew back from where Lina and Spark stood, creating a pocket of breathable air in the heart of the inferno. The heat became bearable. The smoke thinned.

"How—" Finn's voice came from somewhere behind her, rough with smoke. "How are you doing that?"

Lina didn't know. She only knew that Spark was calm now, that the bond between them was burning steady and true, and that somehow, impossibly, they were still alive.

"We need to go," she said. "Now. Before the fire closes in again."

She climbed onto Spark's back—something she had never done before, something they had never tried—and reached down for Finn. He hesitated for only a moment before taking her hand and pulling himself up behind her.

"Hold on," Lina said.

Spark's wings spread wide, and they rose.

They flew through smoke and fire, through darkness and light.

Lina clung to Spark's neck, feeling the powerful beat of wings beneath her, the rush of wind and heat against her face. Behind her, Finn held on with grim determination, his arms wrapped around her waist.

Below them, the Pinewild burned.

The fire had spread beyond the clearing, racing through the forest with terrible speed. Trees that had stood for centuries became torches, their branches exploding with flame, their trunks cracking and falling. The hunters were gone—fled or consumed, Lina didn't know and couldn't bring herself to care.

All she could think about was what they had done. What she had done.

The forest is burning because of us. Because of Spark. Because I couldn't control her.

Through the bond, she felt Spark's guilt—heavy, crushing, a mirror of her own. The dragon had acted on instinct, on the desperate need to protect, and the result was destruction on a scale neither of them had imagined.

"East," Finn shouted over the wind. "The mountains. We can't stop now."

He was right. The fire was spreading westward, toward the village—toward her mother, toward everyone she had ever known. But there was nothing she could do to stop it. Nothing except flee, and hope, and try to survive.

Spark banked east, her wings catching an updraft, and they climbed higher into the night sky. The Highspine Mountains rose before them, dark shapes against the stars, their snow-capped peaks gleaming in the moonlight.

Behind them, the forest burned. The glow lit the horizon like a false dawn, orange and angry, a wound in the darkness that would take years to heal.

Lina didn't look back.

She couldn't.

They landed in a mountain clearing as dawn broke over the peaks.

Spark was exhausted—Lina could feel it through the bond, the deep weariness that came from flying further and harder than she ever had before. The dragon collapsed onto the rocky ground the moment they dismounted, her wings folding tight against her sides, her breathing heavy and labored.

Lina knelt beside her, running her hands over Spark's scales, checking for injuries. There were none that she could see—just exhaustion, and guilt, and the same terrible weight that pressed down on Lina's own chest.

"You saved us," she said quietly. "You know that, right? If you hadn't started that fire, they would have caught us."

Spark made a sound—low, mournful. Through the bond, Lina felt the dragon's response: *But I couldn't stop it. I tried to protect you, and I destroyed everything.*

"I know." Lina pressed her forehead against Spark's neck. "I know. But we're alive. And that has to count for something."

Finn stood at the edge of the clearing, looking back the way they had come. From here, they could see the Pinewild—or what was left of it. Smoke rose in great columns against the brightening sky, and even from miles away, Lina could see the orange glow of flames still burning.

"The village," she said. "Do you think—"

"The wind was blowing east." Finn's voice was flat, exhausted. "Away from the coast. The fire should burn itself out before it reaches the village." He paused. "Should."

It wasn't a guarantee. It wasn't even close to a guarantee. But it was all they had.

Lina stood and walked to where Finn was standing. Together, they watched the smoke rise against the dawn.

"I couldn't control her," Lina said finally. "When she started breathing fire, I couldn't make her stop. I tried, but—"

"You did make her stop." Finn turned to look at her. "You called her down. You calmed her. You created that... that pocket of safety in the middle of the inferno." His expression was strange—wonder, maybe, or something close to it. "I've never seen anything like that. The bond between you—it's stronger than anything I've read about, anything I've been taught."

"It wasn't enough."

"It kept us alive." Finn's voice was firm. "And it will keep us alive again, if we give it the chance. But you're right—it wasn't enough. Not yet." He paused. "You need to learn how to use it. How to guide her, help her control her fire, so this doesn't happen again."

Lina looked back at Spark. The dragon had lifted her head, watching them with those knowing amber eyes.

"Can you teach me?"

"I can teach you what I know. But honestly?" Finn shook his head slowly. "I think you're already learning things I never could. The bond, the connection—that's not something that comes from training. That's something you have to figure out together."

Together. Lina felt the word settle into her, felt Spark's response through the bond—agreement, determination, the fierce resolve to be better, to do better, to never let fear and rage cause such destruction again.

She had spent her whole life running from danger. Hiding. Staying small and invisible and hoping the threats would pass her by.

But she couldn't run anymore. She couldn't hide. The hunters had found them, the forest was burning, and everyone who had seen them fly away on dragonback would know what she was.

A dragon keeper. A traitor to the crown. A girl who had chosen fire over safety.

And if running wasn't an option anymore, there was only one choice left.

She would fight.

Not the way the king fought—with fear and destruction and the crushing weight of power over others. She would fight the way Spark had tried to fight: to protect. To defend. To keep safe the things that mattered.

She just had to learn how to do it without burning the world down in the process.

Lina turned away from the smoke and the fire and the ruin of everything she had known. She walked back to Spark, knelt beside her dragon, and placed her hand on those warm, dark scales.

"We're going to learn," she said. "Both of us. We're going to figure this out."

Through the bond, Spark's response was immediate and certain: *Together.*

"Together," Lina agreed.

And as the sun rose over the mountains, casting long shadows across the snow, she felt something new kindling in her chest. Not fear. Not guilt. Not the desperate hope that had sustained her for so long.

Something fiercer. Something that burned.

A flame that would not be hidden anymore.

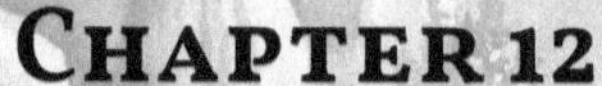

CHAPTER 12

THE HOLLOW MOUNTIAN

The Highspine Mountains were colder than Lina had imagined.

She had seen them from a distance her whole life—those distant peaks rising against the eastern sky, white-capped and mysterious. But seeing them was nothing like being among them. The wind cut through her clothes like knives. The air was thin, each breath a struggle. And the snow—endless, relentless snow—covered everything in a blanket of white that made her eyes ache.

They had been climbing for two days.

After that first desperate flight from the burning forest, Spark had carried them as far as she could—up into the foothills, beyond the reach of the king's soldiers, into territory that belonged to no one but the wind and the stone. But even dragons had limits. By the second morning, Spark was too exhausted to fly, and they had continued on foot, following paths that Finn seemed to know by instinct.

"How much farther?" Lina asked. Her voice came out thin, scraped raw by the cold.

"Not far." Finn was ahead of her on the narrow trail, his shoulders hunched against the wind. He had barely spoken since they entered the mountains—just short directions, occasional warnings about loose rocks or hidden ice. Something was weighing on him, but every time Lina tried to ask, he deflected.

Spark walked beside her, close enough that Lina could feel the warmth radiating from her scales. The dragon had grown again—Lina was certain of it. Her head now reached Lina's shoulder, and her wings, when folded, rose above her back like dark sails. She was too big to hide anymore. Too big to pretend she was anything other than what she was.

Through the bond, Lina felt Spark's weariness, her hunger, her quiet determination to keep moving despite everything. And beneath it all, a thread of something else—curiosity, maybe, or recognition. As if these mountains meant something to her.

"She knows this place," Lina said.

Finn glanced back. "What?"

"Spark. She recognizes it somehow. I can feel it through the bond."

Finn was quiet for a moment. Then: "These mountains were dragon territory, once. Nesting grounds, gathering places. Before the purge, dragons came here from all over Frostmark." He paused on the trail, looking up at the peaks rising around them. "Maybe some part of her remembers. Dragons carry their history in their blood."

Lina looked at Spark—at this creature who had hatched in her arms, who had never known the world before the hunts, who had spent her entire life hiding. And yet something in her recognized these ancient stones, these frozen paths, this place where her kind had once been free.

"Come on," Finn said. "We're almost there."

The Ash Caves appeared without warning.

One moment they were climbing through a narrow pass, the stone walls rising sheer on either side. The next, the path opened into a hidden valley—and there, carved into the black volcanic rock of the mountainside, were the caves.

Dozens of them. Maybe hundreds. Dark openings of various sizes, some barely large enough for a person, others wide enough to admit a dragon twice Spark's size. Steam rose from somewhere deep within the mountain, filling the valley with warmth that seemed impossible in this frozen place.

"The Ash Caves," Finn said. "One of the last safe places in Frostmark. The king's soldiers don't come here—the paths are too dangerous, and they think the caves collapsed years ago." He started down the slope toward the nearest entrance. "Sera brought me here once, when I was younger. Before she—" He stopped, shook his head. "It doesn't matter. We'll be safe here, at least for a while."

Spark moved past them both, drawn toward the caves with an eagerness that surprised Lina. The dragon's weariness seemed to fall away as she approached the dark openings, her head lifting, her nostrils flaring.

Through the bond, Lina felt it—warmth, recognition, the sense of coming home to a place you'd never been but somehow always knew.

"She feels them," Lina said softly. "Other dragons. They've been here."

"Been here?" Finn's voice was strange. "Lina, they're still here."

The cave was warm—warmer than anywhere Lina had been since leaving her mother's longhouse.

Heat rose from deep within the mountain, turning the volcanic stone beneath her feet almost hot to the touch. The walls glowed faintly in places, veins of something mineral catching the dim light and casting it back in soft oranges and reds.

And everywhere, there were signs of dragons.

Claw marks on the stone. Scorch marks on the ceiling. Nests of ash and bone tucked into alcoves, some ancient and abandoned, others showing signs of recent use. The deeper they went, the more Lina felt the presence of other creatures—not threatening, exactly, but watchful. Aware.

"How many?" she asked.

"I don't know exactly." Finn moved carefully through the passage, his hand trailing along the wall. "When I was here before, there were maybe a dozen. Survivors from the early purges, dragons too old or too clever to be caught. But that was three years ago."

Three years. Lina tried to imagine spending three years hiding in these caves, watching the world outside grow more and more dangerous, knowing that any attempt to leave might mean death.

"Why didn't you tell me about this place before?"

Finn stopped walking. When he turned to face her, his expression was difficult to read in the dim light.

"Because I hoped we wouldn't need it," he said. "Because the dragons here... they're not like Spark. They've been hunted, hurt, betrayed. They don't trust humans anymore—not even the ones trying to help them." He paused. "And because there's something else I haven't told you. Something I should have said before we left the village."

Lina felt a chill that had nothing to do with the cold outside. "What?"

Finn was quiet for a long time. When he spoke, his voice was low, heavy with something that sounded like grief.

"The dragons in these caves—they're not the only survivors. There are others. Captured ones." He met her eyes. "The king doesn't just kill dragons, Lina. He keeps some of them alive. Imprisoned. In the dungeons beneath Ironhold Keep."

The words hung in the air between them.

Imprisoned. Lina turned the word over in her mind, trying to make sense of it. She had always assumed the hunts meant death—that every dragon caught was killed, burned, destroyed. The executions at Ironhold. The burned Windrunner in the forest. The Ashback that had died in chains while the king watched.

"Why?" she asked. "Why would he keep them alive?"

"Power." Finn's voice was bitter. "Control. Some dragons are worth more alive than dead—the rare ones, the powerful ones. He keeps them in chains beneath the fortress, starves them until they're too weak to fight, uses them as symbols of his dominance." He paused. "And sometimes, when he wants to make a point, he brings one out for a public execution. A reminder of what happens to creatures that defy him."

Lina thought of the Ashback at Ironhold. Twenty men to bring it down, the traders had said. Chains and nets and sound-traps.

"How long have you known about this?"

"Since I was twelve." Finn looked away. "Sera—the elder who trained me—she tried to free them once. Led a group of trainers into the fortress, thought they could break the locks and get the dragons out before anyone noticed." His jaw tightened. "She was wrong. The king's guards caught them before they reached the dungeons. Most of them were executed. Sera escaped, barely, but she was never the same after. She spent the next five years teaching me everything she knew, and then one day she just... disappeared. Left a note saying she was going back. That she couldn't live knowing those dragons were suffering while she did nothing."

"And?"

"And I never saw her again." Finn's voice was flat. "That was two years ago. I assume she's dead."

Lina stood in the warm darkness of the cave, surrounded by the signs of dragons past and present, and felt something shift inside her.

She had thought escape was enough. Had thought that if they could just get Spark to safety, just hide long enough for the danger to pass, everything would be all right. But the danger wasn't going to pass. The king wasn't going to stop hunting. And somewhere in the depths of Ironhold Keep, dragons were chained in darkness, waiting for a rescue that might never come.

"How many?" she asked. "How many dragons does he have?"

"I don't know exactly. The last count Sera had was eight, but that was years ago. Could be more now. Could be fewer." Finn's expression was unreadable. "Why?"

"Because I'm thinking about what you said. About escape not being enough."

"Lina—"

"You brought us here because it's safe." She looked around the cave—at the warm stone, the hidden passages, the evidence of dragons who had survived by hiding from the world. "But safe isn't the same as free. These dragons, the ones in this cave—they're alive, but they're trapped. And the ones in Ironhold are worse than trapped. They're suffering."

"I know." Finn's voice was tight. "Don't you think I know that? I've thought about nothing else for two years. But what can we do? We're two people and one dragon. The king has an army, a fortress, years of experience hunting our kind. Sera tried to fight back, and it destroyed her."

"Sera went alone."

"She had a group. Trained fighters. People who knew what they were doing." Finn shook his head. "And they still failed. What makes you think we'd do any better?"

Lina didn't have an answer. Not yet. But through the bond, she felt Spark pressing close, and she thought about what Finn had said earlier—that these mountains had once been dragon territory. That dragons came here from all over Frostmark.

"You said there are dragons here," she said slowly. "Survivors. A dozen, maybe more."

"Yes."

"And in Ironhold, there are more. Imprisoned."

"Yes."

"So we're not alone." Lina looked at him. "We're not two people and one dragon. We're two people and maybe a dozen dragons who have every reason to want the king defeated."

Finn stared at her. "You're talking about war."

"I'm talking about freedom." Lina felt the word settle into her bones. "For Spark. For the dragons in this cave. For the ones in chains beneath Ironhold." She paused. "Sera tried to save them by sneaking in. That didn't work. Maybe the answer isn't sneaking. Maybe the answer is giving the dragons a reason to save themselves."

They made camp in one of the smaller caves.

Spark curled around Lina like a protective wall, her scales warm against the cold stone. Finn sat across from them, his back against the cave wall, his expression troubled.

"Even if you're right," he said finally, "even if the dragons here would help—they don't trust humans. I told you that. After everything they've been through, they won't follow us into battle just because we ask."

"Then I won't ask." Lina stroked the ridge above Spark's eyes, feeling the dragon's contentment flow through the bond. "I'll show them."

"Show them what?"

"That it's possible. That humans and dragons can work together. That not all of us are hunters or enemies." She looked at Spark, at the dragon who had chosen her, who trusted her despite everything the world had taught her kind about humans. "Spark trusted me before she had any reason to. Maybe these dragons can learn to trust again, too."

"And if they can't?"

"Then at least we tried." Lina met his eyes. "But I'm not going to hide in these caves while other dragons suffer. I'm not going to spend the rest of my life running from the king's soldiers, waiting for them to find us. If escape isn't enough—if it's never going to be enough—then we have to do something more."

Finn was quiet for a long time. The firelight flickered across his face, casting shadows that made him look older than his years.

"You've changed," he said at last. "Since the first day I met you."

"Have I?"

"The Lina I met in the forest—she was scared. Uncertain. She wanted someone else to tell her what to do." He paused. "You're not that person anymore."

Lina thought about the girl who had found an egg in the cave, who had hidden it and worried over it and never quite believed she was doing the right thing. That girl seemed very far away now.

"Maybe," she said. "Or maybe I'm just scared of different things now."

"Like what?"

She looked at Spark, at the dragon who had become the center of her world. "Like living a life where I never try to make things better. Like hiding so well that I forget how to fight." She paused. "Like being safe while others suffer."

Through the bond, she felt Spark's response—agreement, pride, fierce and unwavering love. *We are the same*, the feeling said. *We will not hide while others burn.*

"Tomorrow," Finn said quietly, "we'll talk to the dragons in the caves. See if any of them will listen." He paused. "I'm not saying I agree with this plan. I'm not saying it will work. But—" He stopped, shook his head. "You're right about one thing. Escape isn't enough. It never was."

It wasn't agreement. Not really. But it was a start.

Lina leaned back against Spark's warmth and closed her eyes. Outside the cave, the wind howled through the mountain passes, and somewhere far to the west, a forest still burned. But here, in this hidden place, she felt something she hadn't felt in a long time.

Not hope, exactly. Something fiercer than hope.

Purpose.

The king had imprisoned dragons. Had broken them, starved them, used them as symbols of fear.

And now, for the first time, someone was going to try to set them free.

CHAPTER 13

BROKEN WINGS

The first dragon they found was dying.

Lina saw him in a chamber deep within the caves—a Frostscale, according to Finn, though his scales had lost most of their color. Where they should have been pale blue and silver, they were gray, dull, like ice that had forgotten the sky. He lay curled against the far wall, his massive body taking up half the chamber, his breathing shallow and labored.

But it was his eyes that made Lina stop in the entrance, her heart clenching.

They were open. Aware. And completely, utterly empty.

"His name is Shard," Finn said quietly. He stood beside her, his face tight with something between grief and anger. "He was one of the first dragons the king captured. Spent six years in the dungeons beneath Ironhold before he escaped."

"Six years?" Lina couldn't imagine it. Six years in chains, in darkness, alone.

"He had a bond once. A trainer from one of the northern villages—they were Flame-Bound for almost a decade." Finn's voice was flat, controlled. "The king executed her in front of him. Made him watch. And then kept him alive afterward, because a broken Frostscale was worth more than a dead one."

Lina felt sick. Through her bond with Spark, she could sense her dragon's distress—a deep, instinctive horror at what had been done to this creature. Spark pressed close to her side, making a low, mournful sound.

"When a Flame-Bind breaks," Finn continued, "the dragon loses something. The ability to trust, to connect. They become... this." He gestured toward Shard. "Alive, but not living. Present, but not there."

Lina took a step into the chamber. Shard didn't react—didn't lift his head, didn't shift his gaze, didn't acknowledge her presence at all. It was like approaching a statue, something carved from stone and forgotten.

"Can he be healed?"

"I don't know." Finn's admission was quiet. "The old texts say a broken bond can't be repaired. But they also say a lot of things that turned out to be wrong."

Lina knelt a few feet from Shard's head. Up close, she could see the scars—lines of white cutting across his faded scales, marks left by chains and fire and things she didn't want to imagine. His flame, when she looked for it, was barely visible in his throat. A dying ember where there should have been a blaze.

"I'm sorry," she whispered. "I'm so sorry for what they did to you."

Shard didn't respond. But through her bond with Spark, Lina felt something—the faintest flicker of awareness, like a candle glimpsed through fog. He was still in there, somewhere. Buried beneath years of pain and loss, but not entirely gone.

"There are more," Finn said. "Others who escaped, others who were never caught. Some are like Shard—too damaged to recover. But some..." He paused. "Come. I'll show you."

The deeper caves held more dragons than Lina had expected.

She counted as they walked—past chambers and alcoves, past nests of ash and bone, past eyes that watched from the darkness with varying degrees of wariness and hope. Fourteen dragons in total. Some were ancient, their scales thick with age. Others were young, barely older than Spark. All of them bore marks of the king's cruelty—scars, missing scales, wings that didn't fold quite right.

And all of them had that same dimness in their flames. That same grief burning low in their throats.

"This is Ember," Finn said, stopping before a smaller chamber. Inside, an Emberwing lay curled around what looked like a nest—but the nest was empty, the space where eggs should have been filled only with cold stone. "She was a mother, once. The hunters took her clutch. Smashed three eggs before she could stop them. The fourth—" He stopped.

"What happened to the fourth?"

"They took it. To Ironhold. The king keeps eggs sometimes, raises the hatchlings in captivity so they never know freedom." Finn's voice was bitter. "Dragons born in chains don't fight. They don't resist. They just... exist. Tools for the king to use."

Lina thought of Spark—of the egg she had found in the cave, abandoned but not forgotten. Hidden, Finn had said once, because dragons hide their eggs when humans become dangerous.

Had Spark's mother been like Ember? Had she hidden her egg to save it from the hunters, only to be caught herself?

Through the bond, she felt Spark's response—not words, but feeling. Sorrow. Recognition. The weight of understanding something terrible about the world she had been born into.

"Show me the rest," Lina said. Her voice came out harder than she intended. "I want to see all of it."

By the time they finished, Lina felt like she had aged a decade.

She had seen dragons with burns that would never heal—scars from the fire nets the hunters used. She had seen dragons missing limbs, wings, tails. She had seen a young Windrunner who flinched at every sound, his body locked in permanent terror from the sound-traps that had been used to capture him.

And she had seen the flames. Dying flames in every throat, guttering like candles in the wind. Trust broken. Hope extinguished. Life reduced to mere survival.

"This isn't just hunting," she said finally. They were back in the main chamber now, the warm heart of the caves where steam rose from cracks in the floor. Spark was pressed against her side, and Lina drew strength from the bond between them—from the steady flame that still burned in her dragon's throat. "This is something else. Something worse."

"It's systematic," Finn said. He sat across from her, his back against the stone wall, his face half-hidden in shadow. "That's what Sera used to say. The king doesn't just want dragons dead—he wants them broken. He wants to prove that they can be controlled, dominated, destroyed in spirit even if their bodies survive."

"Why?"

"Because broken dragons are useful." The bitterness in Finn's voice was sharp enough to cut. "A dragon that's been starved and beaten long enough will do what it's told. It will fight when commanded, burn what needs burning. The king parades them at executions, uses them to terrorize villages that resist his rule. A cowed dragon is more valuable than a dead one."

Lina thought of the Ashback at Ironhold—the great dragon that had been executed while the king watched. Had it been like Shard once? Had it fought and hoped and loved, before years of captivity ground it down to nothing?

"And no one stops him," she said. "No one tries to fight back."

"People have tried." Finn met her eyes. "Sera. Others before her. They all failed. The king has an army, a fortress, years of experience. And most people—" He shook his head. "Most people are too afraid. Or they believe the propaganda. Or they just don't care about what happens to creatures they've been taught are monsters."

"But you care."

"Yes." The word was simple, certain. "I care. But caring isn't enough. I've spent three years caring, and nothing has changed.

The hunts continue. The dragons suffer. And every year, there are fewer of us left."

Lina looked around the chamber—at the warm stone, the rising steam, the evidence of dragons who had survived against all odds. Fourteen dragons in this cave. An unknown number imprisoned at Ironhold. And beyond that, how many more? How many eggs smashed, how many hatchlings killed, how many bonds broken before they could form?

"One dragon can't matter," she said slowly. "That's what I told myself, when I found Spark. I thought—if I can just save this one, keep her safe, maybe that will be enough." She paused. "But it's not about one dragon, is it? It never was."

"No," Finn agreed. "It's not."

"This is systemic." Lina felt the word settle into her, heavy with meaning. "The king isn't afraid of one dragon. He's afraid of what dragons represent. Freedom. Power that can't be controlled. The possibility that there's something in this world stronger than his fear." She looked at Finn. "That's why he breaks them. Not just to use them—to prove that they can be broken. To show everyone that nothing escapes his control."

"Yes."

"Then that's what we have to fight." Lina's voice was steady, certain. "Not just the hunters, not just the soldiers. The system itself. The belief that dragons are monsters, that fear is the only way to be safe, that breaking something beautiful is the same as winning."

That night, Lina dreamed of chains.

She was in a dark place—stone walls pressing close, the smell of smoke and old blood heavy in the air. Around her, dragons lay in the darkness, their flames guttering, their eyes empty. She walked among them like a ghost, reaching out to touch scales that were cold instead of warm, feeling the absence where fire should have burned.

And then she saw Spark.

Her dragon was chained to the wall, iron wrapped around her neck, her wings, her legs. Her scales had gone gray, her flame extinguished, her eyes as empty as Shard's. She looked at Lina without recognition, without hope, without anything at all.

Lina woke with a scream caught in her throat.

She was in the cave, surrounded by warmth and stone. Spark was beside her, very much alive, her flame burning steady in her throat. Through the bond, Lina felt her dragon's concern—the immediate, instinctive response to her distress.

Safe, Spark's presence said. *You're safe. I'm here.*

Lina wrapped her arms around Spark's neck and held on, feeling the warmth of her scales, the steady pulse of her heart. The dream had felt so real—so possible. Because it was possible. That was what the king did. That was what he wanted for every dragon in Frostmark.

"I won't let that happen," she whispered into Spark's neck. "I won't let them break you. I won't let them break any of them."

Through the bond, Spark's response was fierce and certain: *Then we fight. Together.*

Lina pulled back and looked at her dragon—at the copper-black scales, the amber eyes, the flame that burned steady and true. Spark had never known the world before the hunts. She had been born into hiding, raised in fear, forced to flee from the only home she'd ever known. And yet her flame still burned.

That was what the king didn't understand. Fire wasn't just destruction. It was hope. It was warmth. It was the refusal to go dark, even when everything around you was trying to extinguish you.

"Together," Lina agreed. "We fight together."

She found Finn at the entrance to the caves, watching the sun rise over the mountains.

The sky was painted in shades of gold and rose, the light catching the snow on the peaks and setting it ablaze. Beautiful, Lina thought. Even after everything—the flight from the village, the burning forest, the broken dragons in the caves—the world could still be beautiful.

"Couldn't sleep?" Finn asked without turning.

"Bad dreams." Lina came to stand beside him, pulling her cloak tight against the cold. "I dreamed about Ironhold. About what happens to the dragons there."

Finn nodded slowly. "I have those dreams too. Had them for years."

"Is that why you brought us here? To show me what the king really does?"

"Partly." Finn turned to look at her. In the dawn light, he looked younger somehow—and older at the same time. "I brought us here because it was the only safe place I knew. But I also—" He stopped, seemed to gather himself. "I wanted you to understand what we're fighting against. Not just soldiers and hunters. A whole system designed to destroy everything dragons represent."

"I understand now." Lina's voice was quiet but firm. "And I know what I have to do."

"What's that?"

"Free them." She looked at the sunrise, at the world slowly coming alive with light. "Not just Spark. Not just the dragons in these caves. All of them. The ones in Ironhold, the ones in hiding, the ones who've been broken and lost. We have to show them—show everyone—that fire doesn't have to mean destruction. That it can mean freedom instead."

Finn was quiet for a long moment. When he spoke, his voice was careful, measured.

"That's a big goal."

"Yes."

"It might be impossible."

"Maybe." Lina turned to face him. "But yesterday, you told me that escape isn't enough. That hiding and hoping won't save anyone. You were right." She paused. "The king built a system to break dragons. We have to build something stronger—a reason for them to fight back. And that starts here. With us. With Spark. With proving that humans and dragons can still trust each other."

Finn studied her face for a long moment. Whatever he was looking for, he seemed to find it.

"All right," he said finally. "Then let's get to work."

Behind them, in the depths of the caves, fourteen dragons waited—broken, scarred, but not yet defeated.

And somewhere far to the south, in the dungeons beneath Ironhold Keep, more dragons waited in chains.

They had been forgotten. Abandoned. Left to suffer in the dark while the world moved on without them.

But not for much longer.

CHAPTER 14

ACROSS THE SEA OR IN-TO THE FIRE

Three days passed in the Ash Caves.

Three days of learning the paths through the mountain, of meeting the dragons who called this place home, of trying to earn trust that had been shattered long before Lina was born. It was slow work. Most of the dragons would barely look at her, and the ones who did watched with eyes full of suspicion and old pain.

But Spark helped. Having a young dragon at her side, one who was healthy and unbroken, seemed to ease something in the others. They watched Spark move freely around the caves, watched her press close to Lina's side, watched the flame burn steady in her throat. And slowly, cautiously, some of them began to come closer.

Not Shard. The old Frostscale remained in his chamber, motionless, his dying flame barely visible. But others—Ember, the grieving mother; a young Windrunner named Swift; an ancient Ashback called Stone who had survived longer than any dragon Finn had ever heard of—began to watch Lina with something other than fear.

Curiosity, maybe. Or hope.

It wasn't enough. Not yet. But it was a start.

On the morning of the fourth day, Finn asked to speak with her alone.

They walked to the entrance of the caves, where the wind howled through the narrow pass and the world beyond was white with fresh snow. Finn stood with his back to the opening, his arms crossed, his expression troubled in a way Lina had come to recognize.

"I've been thinking," he said.

"About?"

"About what comes next." He paused, seeming to choose his words carefully. "You want to free the dragons at Ironhold. I understand that. I want it too—more than almost anything." Another pause. "But I've also been thinking about what happens if we fail."

"We won't fail."

"You don't know that." Finn's voice was gentle, but there was something beneath it—a weight that made Lina's stomach tighten.

"Sera was smarter than me. More experienced. Better trained. She had a group of skilled fighters, dragons who trusted her, a plan she'd worked on for years. And she still failed. They caught her before she even reached the dungeons."

"So we'll be more careful."

"Careful isn't always enough." Finn uncrossed his arms, and Lina saw that his hands were trembling slightly. "I've spent three years being careful. Hiding. Watching. Doing everything right. And it hasn't changed anything. The king keeps hunting. Dragons keep dying. And everyone who tries to stop him—" He stopped, shook his head.

"What are you saying?"

Finn met her eyes. "I'm saying there's another option. One I haven't mentioned before."

He reached into his coat and pulled out a folded piece of parchment, worn at the edges from handling. He held it out to her.

"What is this?"

"A map. To the western coast, and beyond." Finn's voice was steady now, almost rehearsed. "There are lands across the sea—places the king's reach doesn't extend. Sera told me about them. Havens where the old ways survived, where dragons and humans still live in balance."

Lina unfolded the map. It showed the coastline of Frostmark, and beyond it, a vast expanse of ocean dotted with islands and distant shores. Places with names she had never heard—Windhollow, the Ember Isles, the Dragon's Rest.

"You want to run," she said.

"I want to survive." Finn's voice cracked on the word. "I want you to survive. And Spark. And as many of these dragons as we can convince to come with us." He gestured back toward the caves. "We could take them across the sea, Lina. Start over somewhere the king can't find us. Build something new instead of dying for something old."

Lina stared at the map. The western coast was marked with a small symbol—a ship, she realized. Finn had planned this. Had been thinking about it, maybe for a long time.

"And the dragons at Ironhold?" she asked quietly.

Finn was silent.

"The ones in chains, Finn. The ones being starved and broken. What happens to them if we sail away?"

"We can't save everyone." The words came out rough, pained. "Sometimes you have to choose—the ones you can help, the ones you can't. That's what Sera taught me. That's what kept me alive this long."

"Sera went back." Lina's voice was soft. "Even after she escaped. Even after everything. She went back because she couldn't live with the alternative."

"And it killed her."

"Maybe." Lina folded the map and held it out to him. "But at least she died trying to do something that mattered. At least she didn't spend her last years on some distant island, wondering if she could have made a difference."

Finn didn't take the map.

He stood there, his hands at his sides, his expression torn. Lina could see the war in him—the part that wanted to protect, to preserve, to keep safe the few good things left in the world. And the part that knew, deep down, that safety bought with silence was no safety at all.

"I'm scared," he said finally. The admission seemed to cost him everything. "I've been scared for three years. Ever since Sera disappeared, ever since I realized I was alone, I've been terrified that one wrong move would get me killed. Get the dragons killed. Get everyone I care about destroyed." He looked at her. "And now you're asking me to walk into the heart of the king's power and try to bring it down. How am I supposed to not be scared of that?"

"You're not," Lina said. "You're supposed to be scared. I'm scared too." She paused. "But being scared doesn't mean we stop. It means we're paying attention. It means we understand what we're risking."

"And if we fail?"

"Then we fail trying." Lina felt the words settle into her, solid and certain. "But I'd rather fail fighting for something than succeed at running away. Wouldn't you?"

Finn was quiet for a long time. The wind howled through the pass, carrying snow and ice and the distant smell of the sea. Somewhere deep in the caves, a dragon made a sound—low, mournful, lonely.

"You've changed," he said at last. "Since I first met you."

"You keep saying that."

"Because it keeps being true." A ghost of a smile crossed his face. "The girl I found in the forest—she would never have stood up to me like this. She would have followed my lead, trusted my judgment, believed that I knew best."

"Maybe she would have. But that girl didn't know what I know now." Lina looked back toward the caves—toward Spark, toward the broken dragons waiting in the darkness, toward everything she had promised to protect. "I've seen what the king does to dragons.

I've felt it through my bond with Spark. And I can't pretend that running away will fix anything."

"So what do you suggest?"

Lina turned back to face him. "We go to Ironhold. We free the dragons. And we show everyone in Frostmark that fire doesn't have to mean destruction."

"Just like that?"

"No. Not just like that." She took a breath. "We plan. We prepare. We find a way in that doesn't get us killed in the first five minutes. But we do it, Finn. We have to. Because if we don't—" She paused. "If we don't, then the king wins. Not just this battle, but the war. The idea that dragons are monsters, that fear is the only answer, that breaking something is the same as controlling it. If we run, that idea survives. And it will keep destroying everything until there's nothing left."

Finn stared at her.

She could see him thinking—see the calculations running behind his eyes, the careful weighing of risks and rewards that had kept him alive for so long. He was good at that, she knew. Good at surviving. Good at knowing when to fight and when to flee.

But this wasn't a calculation. This was a choice.

"You're asking me to trust you," he said slowly.

"Yes."

"To follow your lead. Even when I think I know better."

"Yes." Lina met his eyes. "I know you have more experience. More training. More knowledge about dragons than I'll probably ever have. But this isn't about knowledge anymore. It's about what we're willing to risk for what we believe in."

"And you believe in this? Really believe, not just hope?"

Lina thought about Spark—about the dragon who had chosen her, who had trusted her from the very beginning, who had followed her into danger and darkness without hesitation. She thought about the broken dragons in the caves, about the ones in chains at Ironhold, about a world where fire meant fear instead of warmth.

"I believe that we have to try," she said. "I believe that running won't save us—it'll just delay the inevitable. And I believe that somewhere deep down, you know that too. Or you wouldn't have brought me to these caves. You wouldn't have shown me what the king really does."

Finn was quiet for a long time. Then, slowly, he took the map from her hands.

He looked at it—at the distant shores, the promise of safety, the escape he had been planning for who knew how long. And then he folded it carefully and tucked it back into his coat.

"I'm keeping this," he said. "In case we need a backup plan."

"But?"

"But you're right." He let out a breath that seemed to carry years of tension with it. "Sera went back because she couldn't live with running. I told myself she was foolish—that survival mattered more than principle. But I've spent three years surviving, and it hasn't felt like living." He looked at her. "So yes. We go to Ironhold. We try to free the dragons. And if we fail—" A pause. "At least we'll fail for something that matters."

They returned to the caves together.

Spark was waiting at the entrance, her amber eyes bright with questions. Through the bond, Lina felt her dragon's curiosity—the awareness that something important had happened, something that would change everything.

"We're going to Ironhold," Lina told her. "We're going to free the others."

Spark's response was immediate—a surge of fierce joy, of determination, of fire ready to burn. Through the bond, Lina felt her dragon's wholehearted agreement. This was right. This was what they were meant to do.

"The dragons here," Finn said, watching Spark with something like wonder. "Some of them might help. If we can convince them."

"Not convince." Lina shook her head. "Ask. There's a difference."

"Is there?"

"Yes." She looked deeper into the caves, toward the chambers where broken dragons waited in darkness. "The king commands. He controls. He forces dragons to do what he wants through fear and pain. That's not what we're doing. We're offering them a choice—to fight, or not. To risk everything, or stay safe. And we have to respect whatever they decide."

Finn studied her for a moment. "You really are different, aren't you?"

"I'm trying to be." Lina started walking deeper into the caves, Spark falling into step beside her. "I'm trying to be the kind of person worth following. Not because I have power, or knowledge, or a plan. But because I'm willing to trust them the way I want them to trust me."

Behind her, she heard Finn's footsteps following. And though she couldn't see his face, she could feel the shift in the air between them—the moment when teacher became partner, when leader became equal.

She had never asked to lead. Had never wanted it, never believed she was capable of it. But somewhere along the way, in the space between finding an egg in a cave and standing in these ancient mountains, she had become something new.

Not a hero. Not a warrior. Just a girl who had made a choice, and was willing to see it through.

The hidden flame burned brighter in her chest. And for the first time, she didn't try to hide it.

She let it shine.

CHAPTER 15

THE HIDDEN FLAME

Stone came to her first.

The ancient Ashback had been watching from the deepest chamber of the caves, his massive form barely visible in the shadows. Lina had tried to approach him twice before, and both times he had turned away—not aggressive, just dismissive. Uninterested. Whatever faith he'd once had in humans had died long ago.

But on the fifth morning in the caves, as Lina sat with Spark near the entrance watching the snow fall, she heard the scrape of scales on stone behind her.

She turned. Stone stood at the edge of the main chamber, his great head lowered, his eyes—old, golden, veined with something that looked like molten metal—fixed on her face.

"Stone." Lina rose slowly, careful not to make any sudden movements. Beside her, Spark lifted her head, curious but not afraid. "I didn't hear you coming."

The Ashback made a sound—low, rumbling, like distant thunder. It wasn't language, exactly, but Lina felt its meaning through her bond with Spark. A question, colored with something that might have been reluctant curiosity.

Why do you stay?

Lina considered the question. She could have given the practical answer—that they needed allies, that the dragons here could help them free the others. But that wasn't really why she stayed. Not anymore.

"Because you matter," she said simply. "All of you. Not just for what you can do, but for who you are."

Stone's eyes narrowed. Another rumble, deeper this time. Skeptical.

"I know you don't believe me," Lina continued. "I know humans have given you every reason not to trust us. The king, the hunters, the people who stood by and let it happen—" She paused. "But I'm not asking you to trust all humans. Just me. Just this one time. And if I break that trust, you can go back to hating us forever."

The Ashback was silent for a long moment. His flame, when Lina looked for it, was barely visible in his throat—not dying, like Shard's, but banked. Controlled. Waiting.

Then, slowly, he lowered his massive head until his eyes were level with hers.

Through Spark, Lina felt his response. Not trust—not yet. But something else. A door, cracked open after years of being locked.

Show me.

The others came after Stone.

Not all at once—dragons didn't work that way. But one by one, drawn by something they couldn't quite name, they began to emerge from their chambers and gather in the main cavern. Ember, the grieving mother, her eyes still shadowed with loss but her flame burning slightly brighter than before. Swift, the young Windrunner, his body still twitching at unexpected sounds but his curiosity overcoming his fear. A pair of elderly Emberwings who had been hiding in the caves for nearly a decade, their scales faded but their spirits somehow unbroken.

And then, to Lina's amazement, Shard.

The broken Frostscale moved slowly, painfully, his great body scraping against the stone as he dragged himself from his chamber. His eyes were still empty, his flame still dying, his scales still that terrible, lifeless gray. But he was moving. For the first time since they'd arrived, he was moving.

"How?" Finn whispered. He stood beside Lina, his face pale with wonder. "He hasn't moved in months. The other dragons said he just lies there, waiting to die."

Lina didn't have an answer. She only knew that something was pulling at her—a warmth in her chest that had nothing to do with Spark, nothing to do with the bond. Something older. Deeper.

The dragons arranged themselves in a loose circle around her. Fourteen pairs of eyes, all watching. Waiting.

Lina looked at them—at the scars they carried, the pain they'd survived, the flames that burned dim or wild or barely at all. She thought about what Finn had said, what the old trainers believed: that power meant control. That to lead dragons, you had to dominate them.

But that wasn't right. She could feel it now, could see it in the way these broken creatures had gathered around her despite everything they'd suffered. They hadn't come because she was strong. They hadn't come because she could command them.

They had come because she listened.

"I don't have a plan," Lina said.

Her voice echoed in the cavern, small against the vastness of stone and silence. The dragons watched her, unmoving.

"I don't have an army. I don't have weapons or training or years of experience. I'm just—" She paused, searching for the right words. "I'm just a girl who found an egg in a cave and couldn't walk away."

Spark pressed against her side. Through the bond, Lina felt her dragon's encouragement—the steady, unwavering belief that whatever she said next would be exactly right.

"The king wants you to be afraid," she continued. "He wants you broken, silent, too scared to fight back. He thinks if he hurts you enough, burns you enough, chains you enough, you'll forget what it feels like to be free." She looked around the circle—at Stone's guarded eyes, Ember's grief, Shard's emptiness. "But you haven't forgotten. You're here. You're still alive. And that means he's already failed."

A sound moved through the gathered dragons. Not quite agreement, but something close. Recognition, maybe. The acknowledgment of a truth they had stopped believing.

"I'm going to Ironhold," Lina said. "To the king's fortress, where more of your kind are imprisoned. I'm going to try to free them. And I'm asking—not telling, asking—if any of you want to help."

She paused, letting the words settle.

"You don't have to. You can stay here, stay safe, stay hidden. I won't think less of you—none of us will. You've already survived more than anyone should have to survive. But if you want to fight—" She felt her voice strengthen, fed by something she didn't fully understand. "If you want to show the king that his fear isn't strong enough to break you, then I'll stand beside you. Whatever happens."

Silence.

Lina waited. She had said what she needed to say. The rest was up to them.

Stone moved first.

The ancient Ashback raised his head, and for the first time since Lina had seen him, his flame brightened. Not much—not the roaring blaze it must have been in his youth—but enough. Enough to see. Enough to feel.

He made a sound. Through Spark, Lina understood it.

I will go.

Then Ember. The grieving mother lifted her wings, and though her eyes were still shadowed with loss, there was something new in them. Purpose. Direction. A reason to keep burning.

I will go.

Swift, trembling but determined. The elderly Emberwings, leaning against each other for support. One by one, the dragons of the Ash Caves made their choice.

And then, impossibly, Shard.

The broken Frostscale raised his head. His eyes were still empty, his scales still gray, his flame still barely visible. But he made a sound—weak, ragged, barely audible—and Lina felt its meaning pierce through her like light through storm clouds.

I will go. Even if it kills me. Even if I cannot fight. I will not die in this cave, waiting for an end that never comes.

Lina's eyes burned with tears. "You don't have to—"

Shard's response was immediate, fierce despite his weakness. *I choose. For the first time in years, I choose. Do not take that from me.*

Lina nodded, unable to speak. She understood. Choice was all they had left. It was the one thing the king could never truly take away. And Shard had just reclaimed his.

Afterward, Finn found her at the entrance to the caves.

She was sitting on a ledge overlooking the valley, Spark curled beside her, watching the stars emerge from the fading twilight. The air was cold, sharp with the promise of more snow, but Lina barely felt it. Her mind was still in the cavern, still processing what had happened.

"That was remarkable," Finn said. He settled beside her, leaving a respectable distance between them. "I've never seen anything like it."

"I don't know what I did."

"You didn't do anything." Finn's voice was thoughtful. "That's what made it work. You didn't try to command them, or persuade them, or manipulate them into following you. You just—" He paused, searching for the word. "You just were. You showed them who you are, and they chose to trust you."

"But why?" Lina turned to look at him. "They have every reason not to trust humans. We've done nothing but hurt them."

"Not you." Finn met her eyes. "You've never hurt a dragon in your life. You found an egg in a cave and protected it. You raised a hatchling when it would have been safer to let her die. You walked into the king's territory and risked everything to keep her safe." He shook his head slowly. "Dragons sense things, Lina. They feel truth in a way humans don't. And what you showed them tonight—it wasn't power. It wasn't force. It was something else entirely."

"What?"

Finn was quiet for a moment. When he spoke, his voice was soft with wonder.

"Trust," he said. "You trusted them first. You gave them something without demanding anything in return. And that's—" He laughed quietly, but there was no humor in it. "That's the one thing no one has offered them in decades. Maybe ever."

Lina looked out at the valley, at the snow falling soft and silent through the darkness.

She thought about the girl she had been—the one who watched from the cliffs, invisible, forgettable, convinced that courage belonged to other people. She thought about finding the egg, about the fear and uncertainty and the thousand moments when she could have walked away.

She thought about Spark, about the bond that burned between them like a steady flame. About what it had taught her—that strength wasn't about domination, and power wasn't about control.

"Sera used to talk about something she called the Hidden Flame," Finn said quietly. "She said it was the rarest kind of fire—the kind that doesn't burn to destroy. It warms. It lights the way for others. It keeps hope alive when everything else has gone dark." He paused. "I never really understood what she meant. Until now."

Lina felt the words settle into her like embers finding their place in a hearth.

The Hidden Flame.

That was what she carried. Not the power to command, to force, to make others obey. But something quieter. Something that burned without consuming, that led without dominating, that offered warmth instead of demanding surrender.

Courage that didn't seek attention.

Strength that didn't dominate.

Choice that resisted fear.

She had spent so long believing she wasn't strong enough, brave enough, special enough to matter. But maybe that had never been the point. Maybe the point was something else entirely—to be the kind of person worth trusting. To offer protection without expecting reward. To choose courage, quietly, when no one was watching.

Through the bond, she felt Spark's agreement—warm, fierce, absolute. This was who they were. This was what they carried.

Fire that warmed before it burned.

"Tomorrow," she said, "we plan. We figure out how to get into Ironhold, how to free the dragons, how to survive long enough to make a difference." She looked at Finn. "But tonight—tonight I just want to sit here and believe that we might actually win."

Finn nodded. "We might," he said. "We actually might."

They sat together in the cold and the dark, watching the snow fall, while behind them, in the depths of the caves, fourteen dragons slept with flames burning brighter than they had in years.

And in Lina's chest, the Hidden Flame burned steady and true.

Waiting for dawn. Waiting for the world to change.

CHAPTER 16

IRONHOLD

The storm came down from the mountains like a living thing.

Lina had seen winter storms before—the howling winds that swept in from the sea, the snow that buried villages for days at a time. But this was something else. This was a wall of white and gray, lightning flickering in its depths, thunder rolling across the peaks like the voice of an angry god.

"Perfect," Finn said, watching the storm approach from the mouth of the cave. "They won't be able to see us coming."

"We won't be able to see either," Lina pointed out.

"That's what Spark is for." Finn turned to look at her dragon, who stood at the entrance with her wings half-spread, tasting the wind. "Dragons can navigate through storms that would kill a human. Something about how they sense the currents, feel the pressure changes." He paused. "At least, that's what the old texts say."

Through the bond, Lina felt Spark's confidence—steady, certain, unafraid. The storm didn't frighten her. If anything, it called to something deep in her blood, some ancient instinct that recognized the chaos of wind and lightning as a friend rather than an enemy.

"She can do it," Lina said. "She knows the way."

Behind them, in the depths of the Ash Caves, the other dragons waited. Stone had agreed to lead them—to follow at a distance, staying hidden in the storm until the signal came. If things went according to plan, they would arrive at Ironhold just as Lina and Finn freed the prisoners. If things didn't go according to plan...

Lina tried not to think about that.

"Ready?" Finn asked.

She wasn't. Not really. Part of her wanted to stay in these caves forever, safe and hidden, pretending that the world outside didn't exist. That was the old Lina—the one who had spent her whole life avoiding notice, staying small, hoping the danger would pass her by.

But that Lina had died somewhere between finding an egg in a cave and watching fourteen broken dragons choose to hope again.

"Ready," she said.

Flying through the storm was like being swallowed by the sky.

Wind tore at Lina's clothes, her hair, threatening to rip her from Spark's back with every gust. Snow and sleet hammered against her face, so thick she couldn't see more than a few feet in any direction. Lightning cracked across the clouds, close enough that she could smell the burning air, and thunder shook her bones.

But Spark flew on, steady and sure, her wings cutting through the chaos like blades through water.

Lina pressed herself against her dragon's neck, feeling the heat of Spark's scales through her soaked clothes. Behind her, Finn clung with grim determination, his arms wrapped around her waist, his face buried against her shoulder to shield his eyes from the wind.

Through the bond, Lina experienced the storm as Spark did—not as chaos, but as a pattern. The currents of wind, the pockets of calm, the paths between the lightning. Her dragon navigated by instinct and something deeper, some ancient knowledge written in her blood, and Lina let herself trust it completely.

They flew south, always south, the mountains falling away beneath them, the land opening into rolling hills and dark forests. Hours passed—or maybe minutes; time lost meaning in the endless white—and then, suddenly, Spark tilted her wings and began to descend.

Lina saw it through a break in the clouds: Ironhold Keep.

The fortress rose from the earth like a wound in the land. Black stone walls, higher than any building Lina had ever seen. Iron gates that gleamed dully in the lightning's flash. Towers with banners snapping in the wind—the king's standard, a sword through a dragon's skull.

And beneath it all, hidden from view but not from Spark's senses, the dragon prison.

Through the bond, Lina felt her dragon's reaction—a surge of grief and rage and something like recognition. Spark could sense them. The imprisoned dragons, chained in the darkness below. Their dying flames, their broken spirits, their endless suffering.

"I know," Lina whispered, pressing her hand against Spark's neck. "We're going to help them. I promise."

They landed in the shadow of the western wall, where a section of stone had crumbled and been hastily repaired.

"Drainage tunnel," Finn said, pointing to a dark opening near the base of the wall. Water poured from it in a steady stream, swollen by the storm. "Sera's notes mentioned it. It leads to the lower levels—servants' quarters, storage rooms. And eventually, the dungeons."

Lina looked at the opening. It was barely wide enough for a person to squeeze through, and the water rushing from it was black with mud and refuse.

"Spark can't fit," she said.

"No. She'll have to wait here, stay hidden until we give the signal." Finn was already moving toward the tunnel. "Once we free the prisoners, she can lead them out. But getting in—that part, we have to do alone."

Lina turned to Spark. Her dragon's eyes were bright with worry, her flame flickering in her throat. Through the bond, Lina felt the intensity of Spark's reluctance—the desperate desire to stay close, to protect, to never let her human walk into danger alone.

"I'll be all right," Lina said. She pressed her forehead against Spark's snout, feeling the warmth of her dragon's breath. "I need you here. When the time comes, you'll know. You'll feel it through the bond."

Spark made a low sound—reluctant agreement, fierce protectiveness, love that burned like fire.

"I know," Lina whispered. "I love you too."

Then she turned and followed Finn into the darkness.

The tunnel was worse than Lina had imagined.

Cold water rushed around her legs, rising to her waist in places, pulling at her with surprising strength. The walls pressed close on either side, slick with algae and something that smelled like rot. Darkness swallowed everything beyond a few feet, and the only sounds were the rush of water and the distant rumble of thunder from the storm above.

She couldn't see Finn ahead of her, but she could hear him—the splash of his footsteps, the occasional curse when he stumbled. They moved by feel, one hand on the wall, each step a gamble against hidden drops and loose stones.

"How much farther?" Lina called.

"Should be—" Finn's voice cut off with a splash and a muffled oath. Then, after a moment: "Here. I found it."

Lina pushed forward and felt the tunnel widen. Her searching hands found metal—a rusted grate, its bars corroded by years of neglect. Finn was already working at the hinges, his tools clicking softly against the iron.

"Sera taught me to pick locks," he said quietly. "Said it was the most important skill a trainer could have. 'Chains are the enemy,' she used to say. 'And enemies should be defeated.'"

There was a soft click, and the grate swung open.

Beyond it lay a corridor—dry, lit by flickering torches, and empty. The stones were black, veined with iron, and the air smelled of smoke and old blood. This was the heart of Ironhold. The place where dragons came to die.

"We're in," Finn breathed.

Lina looked at the corridor stretching before them. Somewhere down there, dragons waited in chains. Dragons who had been starved, beaten, broken. Dragons who had forgotten what hope felt like.

She had told herself she wasn't ready. Had spent the whole journey doubting herself, wondering if she had any right to be here, to try something so impossible.

But ready or not, she was here. And the only way forward was through.

"Let's go," she said.

They moved through the lower levels like ghosts.

The storm was a blessing—its howling drowned out their footsteps, and the servants who might have spotted them were huddled in their quarters, waiting for the worst to pass. Finn led the way, following the route Sera had mapped years ago, and Lina followed, her heart pounding with every shadow, every distant sound.

They passed storage rooms filled with weapons—swords, spears, the fire nets and iron chains used to hunt dragons. They passed a kitchen where cooks dozed by dying fires. They passed a barracks where soldiers snored through the thunder, their armor hanging on pegs beside their beds.

And then they reached the stairs.

They spiraled down into darkness, carved from black stone, worn smooth by centuries of use. The air grew colder as they descended, and a new smell rose to meet them—the scent of ash and fear, of creatures held too long in chains.

Lina felt it through her bond with Spark—even from this distance, even through stone and iron. The suffering of the imprisoned dragons, radiating upward like heat from a buried fire. Their pain. Their despair. Their fading hope.

"They know we're here," she said softly.

Finn looked at her. "What?"

"The dragons. They can feel us coming." Through the bond, she sensed Spark's confirmation—a resonance, a ripple of awareness passing from dragon to dragon. "They know someone's coming. They just don't know if we're here to help or hurt."

Finn was quiet for a moment. Then: "How do we convince them we're different?"

"The same way I convinced the ones in the caves." Lina started down the stairs. "We don't command. We don't demand. We ask. And we hope they still have enough fire left to answer."

At the bottom of the stairs, two guards stood before an iron door.

Lina and Finn pressed themselves into the shadows, barely breathing. The guards looked bored, leaning against their spears, exchanging muttered complaints about the weather and the late hour. Beyond them, the iron door waited—massive, reinforced, covered in symbols that Lina didn't recognize but that made her skin crawl.

"We need to get past them," Finn whispered.

"I know."

"I could try to—"

"Wait." Lina closed her eyes, reaching through her bond with Spark. Her dragon was still outside, hidden in the shadow of the wall, but she was close enough to hear. Close enough to help.

Through the bond, Lina sent a request—not a command, but a question. A hope.

Spark answered.

Outside, somewhere beyond the walls, a dragon roared.

The guards snapped to attention, their spears raised. One of them said something sharp to the other, and then they were both running—up the stairs, toward the sound, away from the door they were supposed to protect.

"Now," Finn said, and they moved.

The lock on the iron door was complex—layers of mechanisms designed to keep even the cleverest prisoner contained. But Finn's hands were steady, his tools precise, and within minutes the door swung open with a groan of ancient hinges.

Beyond it lay the dragon prison.

Lina stepped through the door and felt her heart break.

The chamber was vast—a cathedral of black stone, lit by guttering torches that cast more shadow than light. And in that darkness, chained to walls and floor and each other, were the dragons.

She counted seven. Some were small, barely larger than Spark. Others were massive, their scales dull with neglect, their wings pinned to their sides by iron bands. All of them bore the marks of captivity—scars, burns, the hollow look of creatures that had given up.

And their flames... barely embers. Barely alive.

"We're here," Lina said, her voice echoing in the darkness. "We're here to help you."

The dragons turned to look at her. Seven pairs of eyes, dull with suffering, flickered with something that might have been hope or might have been fear.

Behind her, Finn was already moving to the nearest dragon, his tools ready. But Lina stood still, letting the dragons see her. Letting them feel her presence—not as a threat, not as a commander, but as something they had forgotten existed.

A friend.

"My name is Lina," she said. "I have a dragon—her name is Spark. We came from the mountains, from a place where dragons still hide. And we came here because we couldn't leave you in chains." She paused. "I know you have no reason to trust me. I know humans have done terrible things to you. But I'm asking you to believe—just for a moment—that it doesn't have to be this way."

The dragons watched. Their flames flickered.

And in the darkness of Ironhold Keep, surrounded by chains and stone and the weight of years of suffering, something began to change.

CHAPTER 17

CHAINS OF FIRE

The first dragon lunged at her before she could draw another breath—one moment Lina stood at the prison's entrance, murmuring words of comfort into the darkness, and the next a massive shape was hurtling toward her, jaws gaping wide, chains snapping taut with a sound like thunder.

The dragon—an Ashback, she realized, black scales and gold veins dulled by captivity—stopped inches from her face. Its chains held, barely, the iron groaning with strain. Hot breath washed over her, smelling of ash and rage, and its eyes blazed with a fury that had been building for years.

Behind her, Finn shouted something. But Lina didn't move. Didn't flinch. Didn't look away.

"I know," she said quietly. "I know you're angry. You have every right to be."

The Ashback snarled, its flame flaring wild in its throat—not dying, not steady, but burning with the chaos of fear and fury. It strained against its chains again, and this time one of the bolts in the wall shifted, stone cracking around it.

"They chained you," Lina continued. Her voice was calm, though her heart was pounding so hard she could feel it in her teeth. "They hurt you. They made you watch others suffer and die. And now I'm standing here, another human, telling you to trust me." She paused. "I wouldn't trust me either."

The dragon's snarl faltered. Just for a moment, just a flicker—but Lina saw it.

"I'm not asking you to trust me," she said. "I'm asking you to wait. Just for a few minutes. Let my friend work on your chains. And then you can decide—fight me, flee, burn this whole place down. Whatever you choose. But give me the chance to set you free first."

The Ashback stared at her. Its flame still burned wild, but something had shifted in its eyes. Not trust—not yet. But consideration. The first crack in a wall that had been building for years.

Slowly, very slowly, the dragon settled back. Its chains clinked as it lowered itself to the ground, still watching her, still wary. But no longer attacking.

"Finn," Lina said, not taking her eyes off the Ashback. "Start with this one."

The work was slow. Agonizingly slow.

Each dragon wore multiple chains—around their necks, their legs, their wings. The locks were complex, designed by craftsmen who understood that a desperate dragon could break almost anything. Finn moved from restraint to restraint, his tools clicking and scraping, sweat dripping down his face despite the cold.

And while he worked, Lina talked.

She moved through the prison, approaching each dragon in turn, speaking softly into the darkness. She told them about Spark, about the egg she had found in a cave. She told them about the Ash Caves, about the other survivors, about Stone and Ember and Swift. She told them about the storm raging outside and the dragons waiting in the darkness, ready to help.

And she told them about choice.

"I'm not your master," she said to a young Emberwing whose scales had gone gray with neglect. "I'm not here to command you. I'm here to ask—will you fight with us? Will you help us end this?"

The Emberwing's flame flickered—still wild, still fearful, but with something else beneath it now. Something that might have been hope.

"You don't have to decide now," Lina continued. "You don't have to decide at all. When those chains come off, you can fly away. You can hide in the mountains where the king will never find you. That's your right." She paused. "But if you want to fight—if you want to make sure no dragon ever suffers like this again—we could use your help."

A click echoed through the chamber. The first chain fell away from the Ashback's neck, clattering to the stone floor.

The dragon didn't move. It sat perfectly still, its eyes fixed on Lina, waiting.

Testing her. Seeing if she would try to command now that it was partially free.

She didn't. She just kept talking, kept moving, kept offering the same thing to every dragon she passed: not orders, but options. Not control, but choice.

The chaos came when the fourth dragon was freed.

It was a Windrunner—sleek and bronze, its long wings crumpled from years of confinement. The moment the last chain fell away, it screamed. A sound of pure anguish, of fury, of years of suffering compressed into a single cry.

And then it attacked.

Not Lina. Not Finn. The walls.

Fire erupted from its throat—wild, uncontrolled, burning so hot the stone itself began to glow. The Windrunner threw itself against the chamber walls, clawing at the black rock, screaming with every breath. Other dragons began to stir, their chains rattling, their flames rising in response to the chaos.

"It's going to bring the whole place down!" Finn shouted. He had stopped working, pressed against the wall, his face pale in the firelight. "Lina, we have to—"

"No." Lina stepped forward, toward the Windrunner, toward the flames. "Keep working. Free the others."

"You can't—"

"Trust me."

She walked into chaos.

The heat was overwhelming, pressing against her skin, stealing the breath from her lungs. The Windrunner's fire roared around her, and for a moment she thought she would burn. Thought this was the end, here in the depths of Ironhold, surrounded by flames and fury and a dragon too broken to know friend from enemy.

But she didn't burn.

Through her bond with Spark, she felt something flow into her—warmth, protection, the echo of her dragon's presence even from outside the fortress walls. And she reached out with that warmth, not to control the Windrunner's fire, but to offer something else. Calm.

"I know," she said. Her voice was quiet, almost lost in the roar of flames. "I know it hurts. I know you want to destroy everything, to burn down the world that did this to you." She took another step forward. "But this isn't the way. This fire—it's not you. It's what they made you. And you're more than that."

The Windrunner spun toward her, its eyes wild, its flame blazing. For a moment, Lina thought it would attack—would burn her where she stood, add her ashes to the centuries of pain this place had witnessed.

But she didn't flinch. Didn't run. Just stood there, in the heart of the fire, and waited.

"You're free now," she said. "Free to choose. And I'm asking you—not commanding, asking—to choose something other than destruction. Choose hope. Choose trust. Choose to believe that it doesn't have to end in fire."

The Windrunner's flame flickered. Wavered. And slowly, like a tide going out, it began to recede.

The dragon stood before her, trembling, its eyes no longer wild but wet with something that might have been tears. Its flame had gone from wild to something else—not steady, not yet, but no longer burning with pure destruction. Something softer. Something almost like grief.

"That's it," Lina whispered. "That's it. You're all right now. You're free."

One by one, the chains fell away.

Finn worked in silence now, moving with desperate efficiency, his tools finding locks and releasing them with practiced ease. And as each dragon was freed, Lina was there—speaking to them, acknowledging their pain, offering them the same choice she had offered the others.

Some of them raged, like the Windrunner had. Their flames burned wild, their fury threatening to consume everything. But each time, Lina walked into the chaos. Each time, she offered calm instead of control, trust instead of command. And each time, slowly, painfully, the dragons chose to listen.

Not all of them. A young Frostscale, barely more than a hatchling, fled the moment its chains were removed—bolting through the open door, up the stairs, into the storm beyond. Lina didn't try to stop it. That was its choice. Its right.

But the others stayed.

The Ashback. The Windrunner. Three Emberwings who moved as a unit, their scales a matching copper dulled by captivity. An ancient Frostscale whose eyes held centuries of memory and pain.

Six dragons, unchained for the first time in years, standing in the ruins of their prison. Their flames burned stronger now—not steady, not fully healed, but no longer dying. No longer the guttering embers of creatures that had given up.

"It's done," Finn said. He was breathing hard, his hands shaking from the work. "That's all of them. Lina, we need to move. The guards will have noticed—"

A sound echoed from above. Footsteps. Many footsteps, moving fast, accompanied by the clatter of armor and the shouts of men.

"Too late," Lina said quietly.

The Ashback moved to stand beside her, its massive body blocking the doorway. The other dragons shifted, forming a rough line, their flames burning brighter. Not attacking—not yet. But ready.

Through her bond with Spark, Lina sent a message: *Now. Bring them now.*

Outside the fortress, in the heart of the storm, she felt her dragon respond. Felt the surge of movement as Spark rose into the sky, felt the answering calls of Stone and Ember and the others as they followed.

The dragons were coming.

And so was the king.

The soldiers arrived first.

They poured down the stairs in a flood of iron and steel, their torches casting wild shadows on the walls. At the sight of the freed dragons, they stopped—a wall of armored men facing a line of creatures they had been taught to fear and hate.

"Hold!" someone shouted. "Hold your positions!"

The dragons growled, a sound like distant thunder. Their flames burned higher, wild with the memory of what these men had done to them. The soldiers raised their weapons—swords, spears, the fire nets that had captured so many of their kind.

"Wait," Lina said. She stepped forward, placing herself between the dragons and the soldiers. "We don't have to do this. We don't have to fight."

"Step aside, girl." The voice came from the back of the group, deep and cold with authority. "Step aside, and we might let you live."

The soldiers parted, and a man walked through.

He was broad-shouldered, gray-bearded, dressed in armor that gleamed black in the torchlight. A crown of iron sat on his head, and his eyes—hard, cold, utterly certain—fixed on Lina with the weight of a man who had never been refused.

King Brann.

"So," the king said, his voice filling the chamber like the rumble of distant thunder. "You're the one who's been causing all this trouble. A child." His lip curled. "I expected something more."

Lina stood her ground. Behind her, the dragons shifted, their flames rising. She could feel their rage, their fear, their desperate desire to burn this man where he stood.

But she held them back. Not with force—she had no force to use. Just with presence. With calm. With the steady certainty that violence wasn't the answer. Not yet.

"I'm not here to cause trouble," she said. "I'm here to end it."

The king laughed—a cold, humorless sound. "End it? Child, you have no idea what you've started." He gestured at the freed dragons. "You think releasing these beasts will change anything? You think they'll follow you, trust you, after everything they've suffered at human hands?"

"They already do," Lina said quietly.

And as if to prove her point, the Ashback lowered its head—not to attack, but to stand beside her. The Windrunner moved to her other side. The Emberwings spread their wings, forming a wall of scales and fire behind her.

Six dragons. Broken, scarred, still healing. But standing with her. Choosing her.

Choosing trust over fear.

The king's eyes narrowed. For the first time, something other than contempt flickered across his face.

Fear.

"Kill them," he said. "Kill them all."

The soldiers charged.

And above them, through the storm and the stone, Lina felt Spark arrive.

CHAPTER 18

THE ASH KING

The soldiers never reached them. The ceiling exploded inward before they could, stone and iron tearing apart like paper as Spark burst through from above. She landed between Lina and the charging soldiers, wings spread wide, flame blazing in her throat. Behind her, through the ragged hole she had torn in the fortress, more shapes descended. Stone. Ember. Swift. The dragons from the Ash Caves, arriving like an avalanche of scales and fire.

The soldiers scattered. Some fled up the stairs. Others pressed against the walls, their weapons forgotten, their faces white with terror. In seconds, the charge had become a rout.

But King Brann didn't move.

He stood in the center of the chaos, his iron crown gleaming in the firelight, his eyes fixed on Lina with something that might have been hatred or might have been recognition. Around him, dragons circled—the freed prisoners joining the newcomers, their flames burning bright, their eyes watching the man who had caused so much suffering.

"Call them off," he said. His voice was steady, commanding, as if he still held all the power in this room. "Call them off, and we can discuss terms."

"I don't command them," Lina said. She walked forward, past Spark, past the ring of dragons, until she stood face to face with the king. "I never did. That's not how this works."

"Then you're a fool." Brann's lip curled. "You've unleashed beasts you can't control. Do you have any idea what they'll do? What they're capable of?"

"I know exactly what they're capable of." Lina held his gaze. "I've seen what your hunters did to them. The chains. The starvation. The executions." She paused. "They're capable of forgiving that. Of choosing peace even after everything you've done. That's what makes them different from you."

Something flickered in Brann's eyes—a crack in the armor of certainty he wore like a second skin. His hand tightened on the hilt of his sword, the way Lina had learned it did when he felt challenged.

"You know nothing," he said. "You're a child. You didn't see what I saw."

"Then tell me."

The king was silent for a long moment.

Around them, the dragons waited. Their flames burned steady now—not the wild fire of rage, but the patient warmth of creatures who understood that this moment mattered. Even Spark had gone still, her amber eyes fixed on Brann with an intensity that seemed to pierce through his armor to the man beneath.

"I was twelve," Brann said finally. His voice had changed—still hard, still cold, but with something beneath it now. Something old and wounded. "When the fire came."

"What fire?"

"The one that destroyed half the capital. The one that killed my mother, my sister, a hundred others." His jaw tightened. "It started at night. No one knows how—a lamp overturned, a hearth left burning, something small that became something monstrous. By the time the sun rose, the eastern quarter was ash."

Lina waited.

"And in the sky above the flames," Brann continued, "there were dragons. Watching. Circling. People said they started the fire. People said they were there to feed on the destruction. People said—" He stopped, drew a breath. "It doesn't matter what people said. What matters is what I saw. Fire. Death. Chaos. And dragons."

"Did you see them breathe fire on the city?"

"I saw enough."

"That's not an answer." Lina's voice was quiet, but steady. "Did you see them attack? Or did you see them watching—the same way they watch storms, and wildfires, and all the other forces they can't control?"

Brann's hand tightened further on his sword. "What difference does it make? They were there. They could have stopped it. They could have—"

"They're not gods." Lina took a step closer. "They're creatures. Living things with their own fears and limits. They can't stop every fire any more than you can stop every storm." She paused. "But you didn't blame the storm, did you? You blamed them. Because it was easier. Because fear needs a target."

"Fear is wisdom," Brann said. The words came out hard, rehearsed—the same phrase that had been preached in his name for years. "Control is mercy. Ash is safety."

"Is that what you tell yourself?" Lina looked around the chamber—at the chains still hanging from the walls, at the scorch marks and bloodstains, at the evidence of years of cruelty. "Is that what makes this acceptable? The Sermon of Safe Ash?"

"It kept my kingdom safe."

"It kept your kingdom afraid." Lina's voice rose for the first time. "That's not the same thing. Fear doesn't protect anyone—it just makes them smaller. Makes them willing to hurt others so they don't have to feel powerless." She gestured at the dragons surrounding them. "Look at them. Really look. Do they seem like monsters to you?"

Brann looked.

For the first time since Lina had met him, the king actually looked at the dragons around him—not as threats to be eliminated, not as symbols of chaos, but as what they were. Creatures with eyes that held pain and memory. Creatures who had suffered under his rule and chosen, impossibly, not to destroy him where he stood.

The Ashback watched him with ancient patience. The Windrunner's flame burned steady, no longer wild. Stone, the oldest dragon in the caves, lowered his massive head until his eyes were level with the king's—and in those eyes, Brann must have seen something. Centuries of memory. Generations of loss. And beneath it all, an offer.

Not forgiveness. Not yet. But the possibility of it.

"They could kill you," Lina said quietly. "Right now, in this moment, they could burn you to ash for everything you've done. You know that."

Brann said nothing. But his hand had fallen away from his sword.

"But they won't. Because that's not who they are." Lina stepped closer still, close enough to see the fear in his eyes—the fear he had built his entire kingdom on, the fear that had driven every hunt and every execution. "Fire doesn't exist to destroy. It exists to warm. To light the way when everything else has gone dark."

"You don't understand—"

"I understand perfectly." Lina's voice was firm. "You lost people you loved, and it broke something in you. So you decided to break the world to match. You told yourself it was protection, but it was revenge. It was fear dressed up as wisdom." She paused. "And it ends now."

"You can't—"

"I'm not going to kill you." Lina shook her head. "That's what you would do. That's what fear does—it destroys what it can't control. But I'm not afraid of you. And neither are they." She gestured at the dragons. "We're offering you something you've never offered anyone. A choice."

"A choice," Brann repeated. The word sounded foreign on his tongue.

"End the purge. Release any dragons still held in your lands. Stop the hunts, the executions, the fear." Lina met his eyes. "And we walk away. No war. No destruction. Just—an end."

"And if I refuse?"

"Then we leave anyway." Lina's voice was calm. "We take these dragons and we fly north, to the mountains where you can't follow. We rebuild. We wait. And eventually, your kingdom crumbles—not because we destroyed it, but because fear can't hold anything together forever. Because people get tired of being afraid."

She watched the words land. Watched Brann struggle with a reality that had no place in his worldview—enemies who didn't want to fight, power that didn't demand submission, strength that looked like mercy.

"You're wrong," he said finally. But there was no conviction in it. Just the hollow echo of a man whose certainty had cracked.

"Maybe." Lina took a step back. "But I don't think so. And I think somewhere, deep down, you don't either."

She turned to walk away—to rejoin Spark, to lead the dragons out of this place of chains and suffering.

That was when Brann drew his sword.

The blade sang through the air.

Lina heard it more than saw it—the whisper of steel, the rush of movement behind her. She started to turn, knowing she was too slow, knowing she would never—

Spark was faster.

Her dragon lunged between them, wings flaring, and the sword struck scales instead of flesh. The blow rang out like a bell, and Brann stumbled back, his weapon vibrating in his hands.

For a moment, everything was still.

Spark stood over Lina, her flame blazing, her eyes fixed on the king with a fury that made the air itself feel hot. The other dragons surged forward, their flames rising, their voices joining in a sound that shook the stones.

"No," Lina said.

The word cut through the chaos like a blade. The dragons hesitated, their flames wavering. Through her bond with Spark, Lina sent a wave of calm, of certainty, of trust.

"No," she said again. She rose to her feet, stepped around Spark, and faced Brann once more. "This isn't who we are. This isn't who I want us to be."

The king stood frozen, his sword still raised, his face a mask of confusion and fear. He had expected fire. Expected death. Expected the monsters he had always believed dragons to be.

Instead, he found a girl who wouldn't let them prove him right.

"You tried to kill me," Lina said quietly. "And I'm still offering you a choice. Because that's the difference between us. You rule through fear. I lead through trust." She held out her hand—not in attack, not in threat. Just an offering. "The purge ends tonight. One way or another. You can be part of what comes next, or you can be left behind. But you don't get to keep hurting them. Not anymore."

Brann stared at her hand. At the dragons surrounding him. At the ruin of everything he had built.

And slowly, like a tree falling in a storm, he let his sword drop.

It clattered against the stone floor, the sound echoing through the chamber like a death knell for an age of fear.

"It's over," Lina said. Not to Brann—to the dragons. To Finn. To herself. "It's finally over."

But even as she said the words, she knew they weren't quite true. The king had fallen, but the fear he had built wouldn't vanish overnight. The wounds he had inflicted would take years to heal.

This wasn't an ending.

It was a beginning.

<h1 style="text-align:center">Chapter 19</h1>

BENEATH THE RUBBLE

Captain Varn came down the stairs.

He was a massive man, nearly as broad as Brann himself, with a face like carved granite and eyes that held nothing but hate. Behind him came more soldiers—not the terrified men who had fled before, but the king's elite guard, the hunters who had spent their lives killing dragons. They wore armor blackened by fire, carried weapons designed to pierce scales, and they looked at the gathered dragons not with fear, but with hunger.

"My king," Varn said, his voice cutting through the chamber like a blade. "Step away from the beasts. We'll handle this."

Brann stood frozen, his sword still on the ground, his face a mask of conflicting emotions. For a moment—just a moment—Lina thought he might refuse. Might tell his captain to stand down, to accept the peace she had offered.

But Brann had spent thirty years building his kingdom on fear. And fear, once it takes root, doesn't let go easily.

"Captain," he said. His voice was hoarse, uncertain—nothing like the commanding tone he had used before. "The situation is... complicated."

"There's nothing complicated about it." Varn's lip curled as he surveyed the dragons. "Beasts in chains, beasts out of chains—they're still beasts. And beasts get put down." He raised his hand, and the soldiers behind him lifted their weapons—crossbows loaded with iron bolts, spears tipped with dragon-killing steel, fire nets ready to throw. "On my command."

"No," Lina said.

She stepped forward, placing herself between the soldiers and the dragons. Behind her, she felt Spark move closer, felt the heat of her dragon's flame rising in response to the threat. The other dragons stirred too—Stone's deep rumble, the Windrunner's anxious hiss, the Ashback's growl of warning.

"Your king surrendered," Lina said. "The war is over."

"My king," Varn said slowly, "doesn't surrender to animals. And neither do I." He turned to his men. "Kill them all. Start with the girl."

The first crossbow bolt flew toward Lina's heart.

Spark caught it in her teeth.

The dragon moved so fast she was almost a blur—lunging forward, jaws snapping shut on the iron bolt inches from Lina's chest. She spat it aside, and the sound of metal clattering on stone seemed to break something loose in the chamber.

The dragons roared.

It was a sound like nothing Lina had ever heard—twenty voices joined in a cry of fury and defiance that shook the very stones of Ironhold. Fire erupted from a dozen throats, not aimed at the soldiers but at the ceiling, the walls, the chains that still hung from the prison's walls. Stone cracked. Iron melted. The fortress itself seemed to groan under the assault.

"Hold!" Varn shouted. "Hold your ground!"

But his men were already breaking. Some fired their crossbows wildly, bolts sparking off scales or vanishing into the smoke. Others threw their fire nets, only to watch them burn to ash before they could touch their targets. The dragons were everywhere—circling, diving, driving the soldiers back with walls of flame that left nowhere to run.

And through it all, Lina stood at the center, untouched.

She could feel everything through her bond with Spark—the rage of the freed prisoners, the fierce joy of the mountain dragons, the ancient fury of Stone as he finally, finally struck back against those who had hunted his kind for decades. It flowed through her like fire, hot and wild and desperately alive.

But it wasn't controlling her. And she wasn't controlling it.

They were choosing. All of them, together. Choosing to fight not for vengeance, but for freedom. Choosing to destroy the chains and the weapons and the walls that had held them captive—not the men who had forged them.

"The exits!" Lina shouted to Finn, who had pressed himself against the far wall. "Get the soldiers out! Give them somewhere to run!"

Finn nodded and moved, darting through the chaos toward the stairs. Behind him, the Windrunner followed—not attacking, but herding, using its wings and flame to drive the fleeing soldiers toward safety rather than cutting off their retreat.

It wasn't a massacre. It was a liberation.

Lina watched in wonder as the dragons worked together—not as a chaotic mob, but as a coordinated force. Stone positioned himself near the main stairway, his massive bulk preventing any reinforcements from descending. The Emberwings worked in pairs, their flames creating barriers that guided the fleeing soldiers toward the exits rather than trapping them. Even the Ashback, whose rage burned hottest of all, aimed his fire at the weapons racks and chain stores rather than at the men who had tormented him.

They were choosing mercy. Every one of them. Despite everything they had suffered, they were choosing not to become the monsters the king had always claimed they were.

Through the bond, Lina felt Spark's pride—not in the destruction, but in the restraint. In the proof that dragons could be more than the fear-stories told about them. This was what she had hoped for. This was what the hidden flame meant.

And the fortress was coming down around them.

The ceiling collapsed in a rain of black stone.

Lina threw herself aside as a massive block crashed down where she had been standing. Dust and debris filled the air, thick enough to choke, and through the bond she felt Spark's desperate search for her—fear and love and the overwhelming need to protect.

"I'm here!" she called out. "I'm all right!"

Spark found her in the chaos, pressing close, wings spread to shield her from the falling rubble. Around them, the dragon prison was tearing itself apart—walls cracking, floor buckling, the weight of centuries of cruelty finally giving way.

"We have to get out," Lina said. "Now."

Through the bond, she sent the message to the other dragons: *Up. Out. Through the hole in the ceiling, into the storm.* The battle was won—there was nothing left to fight for.

One by one, the dragons responded. Stone launched himself upward, his massive body barely fitting through the gap Spark had torn earlier. The Emberwings followed, then the Windrunner, then the others—a stream of scales and fire pouring out of the collapsing fortress into the night sky.

"Finn!" Lina shouted.

"Here!" His voice came from somewhere in the dust, and then he was there—stumbling toward her, his face streaked with soot, his clothes singed but intact. "The soldiers are out. Most of them, anyway. But Lina—the king—"

She looked.

Brann stood alone in the center of the collapsing chamber. His elite guard had fled. His captain had vanished into the smoke. He was surrounded by falling stone and rising fire, and he wasn't moving. Just standing there, watching his fortress—his life's work—crumble around him.

"Leave him," Finn said. "He made his choice."

Lina hesitated. Part of her agreed—this man had caused so much suffering, had built his power on the bones of dragons, had tried to kill her not ten minutes ago. He deserved whatever fate the collapsing fortress delivered.

But that wasn't who she was. That wasn't who she wanted to be.

She remembered what she had told Finn in the caves: We're offering them a choice. That was what made them different from the king. Not power—choice. The freedom to decide who they wanted to be, even when vengeance would have been easier.

If she left Brann to die, she would be making a choice too. A choice to become the thing she had fought against. A choice to let fear and anger decide her actions instead of something better.

"Get on Spark," she told Finn. "Get out. I'll be right behind you."

"Lina—"

"Trust me."

She didn't wait for his response. She was already running—toward the king, toward the falling stones, toward the man who represented everything she had fought against.

"What are you doing?" Brann's voice was hollow, empty. He didn't look at her as she approached—just kept staring at the destruction around him. "Come to gloat?"

"Come to save your life." Lina grabbed his arm. "The ceiling's coming down. We have to move."

"Why?" Now he did look at her, and his eyes were the eyes of a man who had lost everything. "Why would you save me? After everything I've done?"

"Because that's what I do." Lina pulled at his arm, trying to drag him toward the exit. He was heavy, unresisting, dead weight in her grip. "Because killing you doesn't bring back the dragons you murdered. Because your death doesn't heal anyone."

A massive stone crashed down behind them, close enough that Lina felt the impact through her feet. The floor beneath them was cracking, splitting, threatening to give way entirely.

"Move!" she shouted. "Now!"

Something in her voice seemed to reach him. Brann's eyes focused, and for just a moment, she saw the man he might have been—the boy who had watched his mother die, who had let fear consume him, who had built an empire of ashes because he didn't know any other way.

He moved.

They ran together through the collapsing fortress—dodging falling stones, leaping over cracks in the floor, choking on smoke and dust. Lina kept her grip on his arm, kept pulling him forward, kept choosing to save the man who had tried to destroy everything she loved.

Because that choice defined her. Not the killing. Not the vengeance. The mercy.

They burst out of a side passage into the courtyard just as the main tower of Ironhold gave way. It fell with a sound like the world ending—tons of black stone crashing down, burying the dragon prison forever, sealing away the chains and the suffering and the darkness that had lived beneath the fortress for so long.

Lina and Brann stood in the storm, watching it fall. Rain lashed against them, mixing with the ash and smoke, and above them, dragons circled in the lightning-torn sky.

The sight of them—so many dragons, free and flying—was something Lina had never dared to imagine. She thought of the stories her mother used to tell, of the days before the purge when dragons and humans had lived in balance. Those stories had always seemed like fairy tales, remnants of a world that could never return.

But here they were. Flying. Alive. Free.

"Why?" Brann asked again. His voice was barely a whisper now. "I don't understand. Why would you—"

"Because fear is not wisdom," Lina said. "Because control is not mercy. Because ash is not safety." She turned to face him. "Because I'm not you. And I never want to be."

Spark landed beside them, her wings folding against the rain, her flame burning bright. Through the bond, Lina felt her dragon's love, her pride, her absolute certainty that Lina had made the right choice.

Even when it was hard. Especially when it was hard.

The storm began to break as dawn approached.

The rain eased, the lightning faded, and through the thinning clouds, the first pale light of morning began to filter through. The dragons had gathered in what remained of the fortress courtyard—twenty of them now, freed prisoners and mountain survivors standing together for the first time.

Finn found Lina standing at the edge of the ruins, looking out at the kingdom that stretched beyond Ironhold's walls. Villages in the distance, still dark. Roads that led to other settlements, other lives. A world that didn't know yet that everything had changed.

"The soldiers scattered," he said. "Most of them ran when the tower fell. A few stayed to help with the wounded—I think they were more afraid of the dragons than anything, but..." He shrugged. "It's something."

"And Brann?"

"Gone. Walked off into the storm after you talked to him. I don't know where he went." Finn paused. "You saved his life. After everything he did."

"I know."

"Do you regret it?"

Lina considered the question. She thought about Brann's eyes in that collapsing chamber—the emptiness, the loss, the shattered certainty. She thought about what it would have meant to leave him there. To let the stones bury him along with his fortress and his fear.

She thought about her mother, still in the village, waiting for her daughter to come home. About Sera, who had disappeared trying to do what they had just accomplished. About all the trainers and dragons who had died in the years of the purge, whose names she would never know.

Would killing Brann have honored them? Would his death have brought them peace?

"No," she said finally. "Killing him wouldn't have changed anything. The fear he built, the system he created—that doesn't die with one man. We have to dismantle it piece by piece, choice by choice." She looked at Finn. "And we start by being different. By choosing mercy when we could choose revenge."

"You sound like a leader."

"I sound like someone who's tired." But Lina smiled, just a little. "We should get the dragons somewhere safe. The Ash Caves, maybe, or somewhere farther north. The kingdom is going to be chaos for a while—soldiers without orders, villages without protection, people who don't know what to believe."

"And us?"

"Us?" Lina turned to look at Spark, at Stone, at all the dragons who had fought beside her tonight. "We start rebuilding. We show people that dragons aren't monsters. That trust can replace fear." She paused. "It won't be easy. It might take years. But it's the only way forward that doesn't end in more death."

The sun crested the horizon, spilling gold across the ruined fortress and the dragons gathered in its shadow. Twenty pairs of eyes turned toward the light—some ancient, some young, all carrying the weight of what had happened and the hope of what might come.

Stone rumbled something that might have been approval, his golden-veined scales catching the dawn light. Ember stood close to the three young Emberwings, almost maternal in her protectiveness—as if she had found something to care for again after so long. The Windrunner spread his wings to catch the first warmth of the sun, his trembling finally stilled.

They had all lost so much. But they were still here. Still alive. Still capable of choosing what came next.

Lina climbed onto Spark's back and looked out at the world she had helped to change. It wasn't the ending she had imagined when she found that egg in a cave. It was messier, harder, more uncertain than any victory in the stories she had grown up hearing.

But it was real. And it was hers.

"Ready?" she asked.

Through the bond, Spark's answer was immediate: *Always.*

And as the sun rose over Frostmark, the dragons rose with it.

Twenty pairs of wings spread against the dawn. Twenty flames burned bright in the morning air. And at the head of them all, a girl and her dragon flew toward a future they would build together—not with fear, not with force, but with the steady, patient warmth of the hidden flame.

The purge was over.

The rising had begun.

CHAPTER 20

UNBURDENED

One week after Ironhold fell, Lina went home.

She flew in from the east, riding on Spark's back as the sun began its descent toward the sea. The wind was cold against her face—the same wind that had always blown across these cliffs, carrying the smell of salt and pine and the distant promise of winter. Below her, the village emerged from the afternoon mist: the longhouses with their thatched roofs, the docks stretching out into the harbor, the drying racks where fish hung in silver rows.

It looked the same. And yet everything had changed.

Word had spread faster than Lina had expected. By the time the sun rose on that first morning after the battle, runners were already carrying news across Frostmark: Ironhold had fallen. The king's dragon prison lay in ruins. And somewhere in the chaos, King Brann himself had disappeared—some said dead, others said fled, all of them uncertain what it meant for the kingdom he had ruled through fear.

The hunts had stopped. Not because anyone had ordered them to, but because the hunters themselves had scattered when Ironhold fell. Some had thrown down their weapons and walked away. Others had fled to distant settlements, afraid of what the freed dragons might do. A few—a precious few—had come to the Ash Caves in the days that followed, asking if there was a place for them in whatever came next.

Lina had welcomed them. Not because she trusted them—trust would take time—but because she believed in second chances. In choices. In the possibility that people could become more than their fear had made them.

Now, circling above her village, she wondered if her own people would offer her the same grace.

The villagers saw her coming.

She watched them emerge from their homes, their faces turned upward, their hands shielding their eyes against the setting sun. She saw children point and adults gather in clusters, their voices carrying up to her as frightened murmurs. A dragon was approaching their village—for most of them, that had meant death for as long as they could remember.

But Lina also saw something else. She saw old Marta step out of her longhouse, her weathered face creased with something that might have been wonder. She saw the Eriksson children run toward the cliffs rather than away, their voices bright with excitement rather than fear. And she saw her mother.

Kara stood at the edge of the village, where the path led up toward the cliffs. She was alone, her arms wrapped around herself against the cold, her eyes fixed on the approaching dragon with an expression Lina couldn't read from this distance.

"Take us down," Lina said. "Slowly. Let them see us."

Through the bond, Spark sent a pulse of understanding. She began to descend in a wide spiral, her wings catching the light, her copper-black scales gleaming like something out of the old stories. She was beautiful—Lina had always known that—but now, flying openly in the sky above her home, she was something more.

She was proof.

Proof that dragons weren't monsters. Proof that the king's fear had been wrong. Proof that the world could change, if enough people were brave enough to let it.

They landed on the clifftop—the same cliffs where Lina had stood so many times before, watching dragons pass overhead and dreaming of a different life. The wind whipped around them, carrying the scent of the sea, and for a moment Lina just sat there, breathing it in.

Home. She was home.

Her mother reached her first.

Kara climbed the path to the cliffs with a determination that belied her age, her breath coming in short gasps by the time she reached the top. She stopped a few feet from Spark, her eyes taking in the dragon—the scales, the wings, the flame that flickered low and steady in her throat—and then moving to Lina.

"You came back," she said.

"I promised I would."

"You promised you'd be careful, too." But there was no anger in her mother's voice—just a kind of exhausted relief, the sound of someone who had spent too many nights lying awake, wondering if her daughter was alive. "The stories we've been hearing... Ironhold, the king, dragons flying free across Frostmark..." She shook her head. "They said a girl led them. A girl with a dragon of her own."

"They weren't wrong."

Kara looked at Spark again. The dragon held perfectly still, her amber eyes fixed on Lina's mother with an intelligence that was impossible to miss. Through the bond, Lina felt Spark's careful hope—the desire to be accepted, to be seen as something other than a threat.

"She's beautiful," Kara said softly. "I didn't expect... the stories always made them sound terrible. Monsters of fire and rage." She took a tentative step closer. "But she's not, is she? She's just... alive. Like everything else."

"Her name is Spark," Lina said. "And she's the best thing that ever happened to me."

Through the bond, Spark's warmth wrapped around her like an embrace. And when Kara reached out—slowly, carefully—to touch the dragon's snout, Spark leaned into her hand with a gentleness that made Lina's eyes sting with tears.

"Thank you," Kara whispered to Spark. "For keeping her safe."

Spark's flame flickered brighter—just for a moment—and Lina knew her dragon understood.

The village gathered as the sun set.

They came in ones and twos at first, climbing the cliff path with cautious steps, keeping their distance from Spark until they saw that Lina's mother stood unharmed beside the dragon. Then more came—curious children, skeptical elders, young people who had grown up hearing nothing but horror stories about dragons.

Lina spoke to them. Not as a leader—she didn't feel like one, not really—but as the girl who had grown up among them, who had fished in their harbor and mended their nets and watched dragons from these very cliffs.

She told them about finding Spark's egg. About the fear and the wonder and the choice she had made to protect something instead of destroying it. She told them about Finn, about the Ash Caves, about the dragons who had suffered under the king's rule and chosen mercy even when they could have chosen revenge.

She told them about the hidden flame—about courage that didn't need to be loud, about strength that didn't need to dominate. About fire that warmed instead of burned.

"The king taught us that dragons were monsters," she said. "That fire meant destruction. That the only way to be safe was to be afraid." She looked out at the faces around her—some fearful, some skeptical, some starting to hope. "But I've seen what fear does. It doesn't protect anyone. It just makes us smaller. Makes us willing to hurt others so we don't have to feel powerless."

She rested her hand on Spark's neck, feeling the familiar warmth of her dragon's scales.

"The world is different now," she continued. "The hunts are over. Dragons are flying free across Frostmark for the first time in years. And yes, that's frightening. Change always is." She paused. "But it doesn't have to mean chaos. It doesn't have to mean fire from the sky. It can mean something else—something the old stories talked about before we forgot how to listen."

"Balance," old Marta said. Her voice was rough with age, but her eyes were sharp. "The songs used to speak of it. Dragons and humans, living together. Respecting each other."

"Yes." Lina nodded. "Balance. Not dragons ruling over us, not us hunting them to extinction. Just... coexistence. Trust. The understanding that we're all part of the same world, and that world is better when we work together instead of against each other."

The villagers were quiet. Some of them still looked afraid—that wouldn't change overnight, Lina knew. Fear that deep took time to heal.

But others were looking at Spark differently now. Not as a monster, but as a creature. A being with her own thoughts, her own feelings, her own capacity for gentleness and grace.

It was a start.

That night, Lina slept in her own bed for the first time in weeks.

Spark curled outside the longhouse, too large now to fit through the door. But through the bond, Lina could feel her dragon's contentment—the simple pleasure of rest after so much struggle, of safety after so much danger. They were together. They were home. For now, that was enough.

In the morning, there would be work to do. Messages to send to Finn and the dragons in the Ash Caves. Plans to make for the difficult months ahead—helping villages across Frostmark adjust to a world without hunts, without fear, without a king to tell them what to believe. There would be setbacks and struggles, people who couldn't let go of the old ways, dragons who couldn't forgive what had been done to them.

Peace was fragile. Lina knew that better than anyone.

But tonight, lying in the darkness of her mother's longhouse, listening to the wind off the sea and the distant sound of waves against the cliffs, she let herself believe that it was possible. That all of it—the fear, the fighting, the choices that had cost her so much—had been worth it.

Through the bond, Spark sent a pulse of love. Steady, certain, unwavering.

Lina smiled in the darkness and let sleep take her.

She woke to the sound of wings.

For a moment, still caught between sleep and waking, she thought she was dreaming. But the sound grew louder—the beat of multiple wings, the rush of air, the chorus of voices that weren't quite voices but something older, deeper, more primal.

Dragons. Coming from the east.

Lina threw off her blankets and ran outside, her heart pounding. The sky was just beginning to lighten with the first hints of dawn, and against that pale canvas, she saw them: shapes rising from the mountains, growing larger as they approached. Stone's massive silhouette, unmistakable even at this distance. The sleeker forms of the Windrunners. The copper-red glow of Emberwings catching the first light of sunrise.

Spark was already on her feet, her wings half-spread, her flame burning bright with excitement. Through the bond, Lina felt her dragon's joy—the pure, overwhelming happiness of seeing her kind flying free, together, alive.

"They came," Lina breathed.

"Of course they came." The voice belonged to Finn. He emerged from behind the longhouse, looking sleep-rumpled and wind-worn, but grinning. "Did you think they would let you have all the fun?"

"How did you—"

"Stone knew where you were going. They all did." Finn shrugged. "Dragons are connected, remember? When you decided to come home, they felt it. And they decided to follow."

The dragons reached the village in a wave of wind and fire. They circled overhead—twenty of them, maybe more, their scales catching the rising sun in a blaze of color. Stone roared, and the sound echoed off the cliffs like thunder. The Windrunners dove and spun, their long wings tracing patterns in the air. The Emberwings flew in formation, their flames creating a trail of light across the dawn sky.

And below them, the village watched.

Not with fear. Not with hatred. Just with wonder—the wonder of seeing something beautiful, something they had been taught to fear, something they were only now learning to understand.

"This is it," Finn said quietly. "This is what the old world must have looked like. Dragons in the sky. Humans below. Balance."

"Not yet," Lina said. "We're not there yet. This is just the beginning."

"I know." Finn smiled. "But it's a good beginning, don't you think?"

Lina looked at the dragons overhead, at the villagers emerging from their homes, at her mother standing in the doorway with tears streaming down her face. She looked at Spark, her dragon, her partner, her friend, the creature who had changed everything.

"Yes," she said. "It is."

Later that morning, Lina flew.

She climbed onto Spark's back as she had so many times before, feeling the familiar warmth of her dragon's scales, the powerful beat of wings as they lifted into the air. But this time was different. This time, she wasn't fleeing. Wasn't hiding. Wasn't racing toward danger or away from fear.

She was just flying. Because she could. Because she wanted to. Because the sky was open and the world was wide and she had earned the right to be here, visible, seen.

The other dragons flew with them. Stone on one side, steady and ancient. Ember on the other, her grief-dulled scales slowly regaining their brightness. The Windrunners raced ahead, swift and free. The young Emberwings tumbled through the air like puppies, rediscovering the joy of flight after so long in chains.

They flew over the village, over the harbor, over the cliffs where Lina had spent so many hours dreaming of exactly this moment. The wind caught her hair, the same wind that had always blown across this coast—but it felt different now. Warmer, somehow. Fuller. Like it was welcoming her instead of just passing through.

She remembered the girl she had been before all this. Small, invisible, afraid to be noticed. Watching dragons pass overhead and never imagining she might fly beside them.

That girl was gone. Or maybe not gone—maybe just transformed. The fear was still there, buried deep. The uncertainty, the doubt, the small voice that whispered she wasn't strong enough, brave enough, good enough.

But alongside those voices now lived something else. Something that burned steadily and warmed her chest, refusing to go out no matter how hard the wind blew.

The hidden flame.

Not the fire of destruction. Not the blaze that consumed everything in its path. Just a small, steady warmth—the kind that lit the way home in the darkness, that kept hope alive through the longest winters, that reminded her who she was and who she wanted to be.

Through the bond, Spark sent a surge of love. *Together*, the feeling said. *Always together.*

"Together," Lina agreed.

They climbed higher, breaking through a layer of clouds into the pure, golden light of morning. Below them, Frostmark spread out in all directions—mountains and forests, villages and harbors, a kingdom slowly learning to live without fear.

It wouldn't be easy. Nothing worth having ever was. There would be struggles ahead, setbacks and challenges and moments when it all seemed impossible.

But for now, flying through the golden light with her dragon beneath her and her family below, Lina let herself hope.

The purge was over. The balance was returning.

And the hidden flame burned on.

THANK YOU

THANK YOU FOR READING.

If you enjoyed this story, I'd love for you to explore my other novels,
where new worlds, characters, and adventures are waiting for you.
Leaving a kind review on Amazon also makes a real difference.
Reviews help readers discover books like this one and allow stories
to reach the people who may need them most.
Thank you for spending your time in this world. I hope it stays
with you long after the final page.
— *Bryan Hewes*

WWW.SLICKHILLMEDIA.COM
Explore new titles, read blog updates, and join our newsletter
for future announcements and exclusive news.

ABOUT THE AUTHOR

Bryan Hewes is a fantasy author who writes character-driven stories about courage, choice, and the quiet strength it takes to protect what others fear.

His work blends vivid world-building with emotionally grounded storytelling, focusing on ordinary people who find themselves carrying extraordinary responsibility.

When he's not writing, Bryan works in media and publishing, where storytelling, precision, and attention to detail shape his creative process. He is the founder of Slickhill Media, an independent publishing company dedicated to immersive fantasy and youth-focused fiction.

The Hidden Flame is his debut novel and the first entry in an epic fantasy series exploring dragons, loyalty, and what it truly means to be chosen.

Bryan lives in the United States and is always working on the next story.